ALSO BY MARTIN AMIS

FICTION

The Rachel Papers

Dead Babies

Success

Other People

Money

Einstein's Monsters

London Fields

Time's Arrow

The Information

Night Train

Heavy Water and Other Stories

Yellow Dog

NONFICTION

Invasion of the Space Invaders

The Moronic Inferno

Visiting Mrs. Nabokov

Experience

The War Against Cliché

Koba the Dread

HOUSE OF MEETINGS

HOUSE OF MEETINGS

Martin Amis

ALFRED A. KNOPF
NEW YORK · TORONTO · 2007

THIS IS A BORZOI BOOK
PUBLISHED BY ALFRED A. KNOPF
AND ALFRED A. KNOPF CANADA

 Published in the United States by
Alfred A. Knopf, a division of Random House, Inc., New York,
and in Canada by Alfred A. Knopf Canada, a division of
Random House of Canada Limited, Toronto.
www.aaknopf.com
www.randomhouse.ca
Originally published in Great Britain by Jonathan Cape,
a division of the Random House Group Ltd., London, in 2006.

ISBN: 978-1-4000-4455-9
LC Control Number: 2006047397

Library and Archives Canada Cataloguing in Publication
Amis, Martin, 1949–
House of meetings / Martin Amis.
ISBN 978-0-676-97787-5
I. Title.
PR6051.M58H68 2007 823'.914 C2006-905392-8

Manufactured in the United States of America
First North American Edition

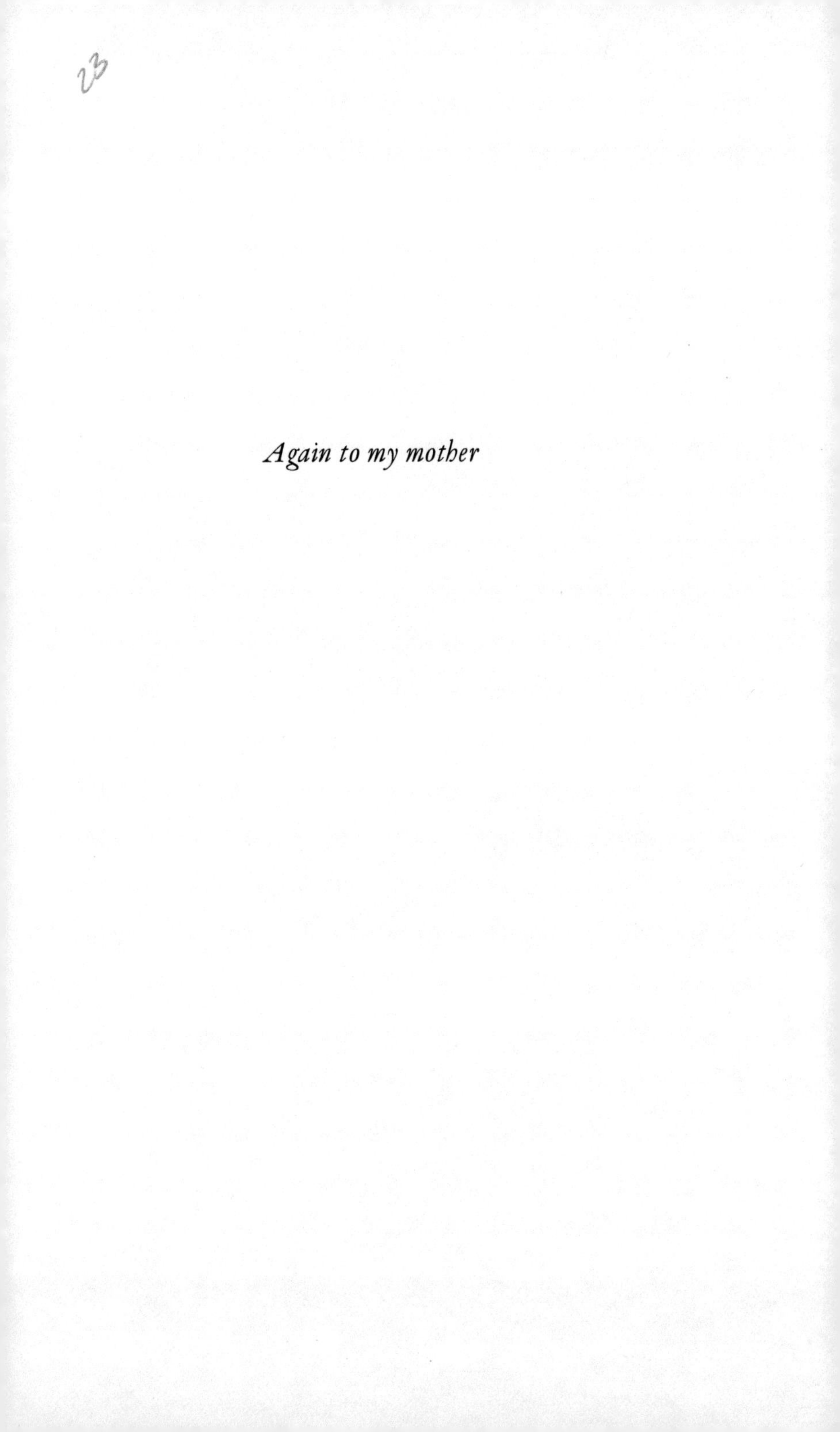

Again to my mother

HOUSE OF MEETINGS

Dear Venus,

If what they say is true, and my country is dying, then I think I may be able to tell them why. You see, kid, the conscience is a vital organ, and not an extra like the tonsils or the adenoids.

Meanwhile, I offer my congratulations. You now join a substantial contingent of young people—those condemned to tout the festering memoirs of an elderly relative. Still, you won't have to go far: the Gagarin Press on Jones Street. Ask for Mr. Nosrin. Do not worry: I won't be going the way of that fuddled deviant we read about, who sent whole rolls of his handiwork to One Hour Photo. Nosrin has been squared (and everything is paid for). Besides, he's a compatriot of mine, so he'll understand. I'd like a print run, please, consisting of a single copy. It is yours.

You were always asking me why I could never "open up," why I found it so hard to "vent" and "decompress" and all the rest of it. Well, with a past like mine, you pretty much live for the interludes when you aren't thinking about it—and time spent talking about it clearly isn't going to be one of them. There was a more obscure inhibition: the frankly neurotic fear that you wouldn't believe me. I saw you turning away, I saw you turning your face away and slowly shaking your lowered head. And this was for some reason an unendurable prospect. I said my fear was neurotic, but I know it to be widely shared by men with similar histories. Shared neurosis, shared anxiety. Mass emotion: we will have to keep returning to the subject of mass emotion.

When at first I assembled the facts before me, black words on a white page, I found myself staring at a shapeless little heap of degradation and horror. So I've tried to give the thing a bit of structure. Inasmuch as I could locate some semblance of form and pattern, I felt less isolated, and could sense the assistance of impersonal forces (which I badly needed). This intimation of unity was perhaps delusive. The fatherland is eternally prodigal with anti-illuminations, with negative epiphanies—but not with unity. There aren't any unities in my country.

In the 1930s there was a miner called Aleksei Stakhanov who, some said, unearthed more than a hundred tons of coal—the quota was seven—in a single shift. Hence the cult of the Stakhanovites, or "shock" workers: canyon-fillers and mountain-flatteners, human bulldozers and excavators. Stakhanovites, very often, were obvious frauds; very often, too, they were strung up by their mates, who hated the ballooning norms . . . There were also "shock" writers. They were taken off the factory floor, in their thousands, and trained to write propaganda in the guise of prose fiction. My purpose is otherwise, but that's how you'd better think of me—as a "shock" writer who is telling the truth.

The truth will be painful for you. It has once again struck me (a subtle laceration, like a paper cut) that my most disgraceful act was perpetrated, not in the distant past, like nearly all the others, but well within your lifetime, and a matter of months before I was introduced to your mother. My ghost expects censure. But make it personal,

Venus; make it your own and not the censure of your group and your ideology. Yes, you heard me, young lady: your ideology. Oh, it's a mild ideology, I agree (mildness is its one idea). Nobody's going to blow themselves to bits for it.

Your assimilation of what I did—this will in any case be a heavy call on your courage and generosity. But I think that even a strict retributionist (which you are not) would be reasonably happy with the way things turned out. It could be objected, and I would not argue, that I didn't deserve your mother; and I didn't deserve to have you in the house for nearly twenty years. Nor do I now seriously fear that you will excommunicate me from your memory. I don't think you'll do that. Because you understand what it means to be a slave.

Venus, I'm sorry that you've gone on minding that I didn't let you drive me to O'Hare. "That's what we do," you said: "We drive each other to and from the airport." Do you realize how rare that is? No one *does it anymore, not even newlyweds. All right—it was selfish of me to decline. I said it was because I didn't want to say goodbye to you in a public place. But I think it was the asymmetry of it that was really troubling me. You and I, we drive each other to and from the airport. And I didn't want a* to *when I knew there wouldn't be a* from.

You are as well-prepared as any young Westerner could hope to be, equipped with good diet, lavish health insurance, two degrees, foreign travel and languages, orthodonture, psychotherapy, property, and capital; and your skin is a beautiful color. Look at you—look at the burnish of you.

PART I

1.

The Yenisei, September 1, 2004

My little brother came to camp in 1948 (I was already there), at the height of the war between the brutes and the bitches . . .

Now that wouldn't be a bad opening sentence for the narrative proper, and I am impatient to write it. But not yet. "Not yet, not yet, my precious!" This is what the poet Auden used to say to the lyrics, the sprawling epistles, that seemed to be lobbying him for premature birth. It is too early, now, for the war between the brutes and the bitches. There will be war in these pages, inevitably: I fought in fifteen battles, and, in the seventh, I was almost castrated by a secondary missile (a three-pound iron bolt), which lodged itself in my inner thigh. When you get a wound as bad as that, for the first hour you don't know whether you're a man or a woman (or whether you're old or young, or who your father was or what your name is). Even so, an inch or two further up, as they say, and there would have been no story to tell—because this is a love story. All right, Russian love. But still love.

The love story is triangular in shape, and the triangle is not equilateral. I sometimes like to think that the triangle is isosceles: it certainly comes to a very sharp point. Let's be honest, though, and admit that the triangle remains brutally scalene. I trust, my dear, that you have a dictionary nearby? You never needed much encouragement in your respect for dictionaries. Scalene, from the Greek, *skalenos:* unequal.

It's a love story. So of course I must begin with the House of Meetings.

I'm sitting in the prow-shaped dining room of a tourist steamer, the *Georgi Zhukov*, on the Yenisei River, which flows from the foothills of Mongolia to the Arctic Ocean, thus cleaving the northern Eurasian plain—a distance of some two and a half thousand versts. Given Russian distances, and the general arduousness of Russian life, you'd expect a verst to be the equivalent of—I don't know—thirty-nine miles. In fact it's barely more than a kilometer. But that's still a very long ride. The brochure describes the cruise as "a journey to the destination of a lifetime"—a phrase that carries a somewhat unwelcome resonance. Bear in mind, please, that I was born in 1919.

Unlike almost everywhere else, over here, the *Georgi Zhukov* is neither one thing nor the other: neither futuristically plutocratic nor futuristically stark. It is a picture of elderly, practically tsarist *Komfortismus*. Below the waterline, where the staff and crew slumber and carouse, the ship is of course a fetid ruin—but look at the dining room, with its honey-gold drapes, its brothelly red velvets. And our load is light. I have a four-berth cabin all to myself. The Gulag Tour, so the purser tells me, never quite caught on . . . Moscow *is* impressive—grimly fantastic in its pelf. And Petersburg, too, no doubt, after its billion-dollar birthday: a tercentenary for the slave-built city "stolen from the sea." It's everywhere else that is now below the waterline.

My peripheral vision is ringed by crouching waiters, ready to pounce. There are two reasons for this. First, we have reached the penultimate day of our voyage, and by now it is massively established, aboard the *Georgi Zhukov*, that I am a vile-tempered and foul-mouthed old man—huge and shaggy, my hair not the downy white of the unprotesting dotard but a jagged and bitter gray. They also know, by now, that I am a psychotic overtipper. I don't know why. I was from the start, I suppose, a twenty-percenter rather than a ten, and it's climbed steadily since; but this is ridiculous. I always had a lot of spare cash, even in the USSR. But now I'm rich. For the record (and this *is* my record), just one patent, but with wide applications: a mechanism that significantly improves the "give" of prosthetic extremities . . . So all the waiters know that if they survive my cloacal frenzies, then a competence awaits them at the end of every meal. Propped up before me, a book of poems. Not Mikhail Lermontov or Marina Tsvetaeva. Samuel Coleridge. The bookmark I use is a plump envelope with a long letter in it. It's been in my possession for twenty-two years. An old Russian, coming home, must have his significant keepsake—his *deus ex machina*. I haven't read the letter yet, but I will. I will, if it's the last thing I do.

Yes, yes, I know—the old shouldn't swear. You and your mother were quite right to roll your eyes at it. It is indeed a charmless and pitiful spectacle, the effing and blinding of an ancient mouth, the teeth false or dropped, the lips licked half away. And pitiful because it is such a transparent protest against failing powers: *saying* fuck is the only dirty thing we can still get up to. But I would like to emphasize the therapeutic properties of the four-letter word. All those who have truly grieved know the relief it eventually brings, to dip your head and, for hour upon hour, to weep and swear . . . Christ, look at my hands. The size of cheese-boards, no, cheeses, whole cheeses, with their pocks and ripples, their spread, their verdigris. I have hurt many men and women with these hands.

On August 29 we crossed the Arctic Circle, and there was a very comprehensive celebration aboard the *Georgi Zhukov*. An accordion, a violin, a much-bejeweled guitar, girls in wenchy blouses, a jodhpured drunk who tried to fake the Cossack dance and kept falling off his stool. I now have a hangover which, two days later, is still getting steadily worse. And at my age, in the "high" eighties, as they now say (in preference to the "late," with its unfortunate connotations), there just isn't *room* for a hangover. Dear oh dear . . . Oh dear oh dear oh dear. I didn't think I was still capable of polluting myself quite so thoroughly. Worse, I succumbed. You know very well what I mean. I joined in all the toasts (a miniature dumpster had been provided for us to smash our glasses into), and I sang all the songs; I wept for Russia, and staunched my tears on her flag. I talked a very great deal about camp—about Norlag, about Predposylov. Around dawn, I started physically preventing certain people from leaving the bar. Later on I did a fair amount of damage to my cabin and had to be moved the next day, in a blizzard of swearwords and twenty-dollar bills.

Georgi Zhukov, General Zhukov, Marshal Zhukov: I served in one of his armies (he commanded a whole front) in 1944 and 1945. He also played a part in saving my life—eight years later, in the summer of 1953. Georgi Zhukov was the man who won the Second World War.

Our ship groans, as if shouldering yet more burdens and cares. I like this sound. But when the doors to the galley blat open I hear the music from the boombox (four beats to the bar, with some seventeen-year-old yelling about self-discovery), and it comes to my ears as pain. Naturally, at a single flicker of my eyelid, the waiters take the kitchen by storm. When you are old, noise comes to you as pain. Cold comes to you as pain. When I go up on deck tonight, which I will do, I expect the wet snow to come to me as pain. It wasn't like that when I was young. The wake-up: *that* hurt, and went on hurting more and more. But the cold didn't hurt. By the way, try crying and swearing above the Arctic Circle, in winter. All your tears will freeze fast, and even your obscenities will turn to droplets of ice and tinkle to your feet. It weakened us, it profoundly undermined us, but it didn't come to us as pain. It answered something. It was like a searchlight playing over the universe of our hate.

Now the boombox has been supplanted by a radio. I hold up a hand. This is permitted. Today saw the beginning of the siege of Middle School Number One, in North Ossetia. Some of the children happened to be watching when the gunmen and gunwomen came over the railway track in their black balaclavas—and they laughed and pointed, thinking it was a game or an exercise. Then the van pulled up and out he climbed, the killer with the enormous orange beard: "Russians, Russians, don't be afraid. Come. Come . . ." The authorities are saying three or four hundred, but in fact there are well over a thousand hostages—children, parents, teachers. And why is it that we are already preparing ourselves for something close to the worst possible outcome? Why is it that we are already preparing ourselves for the phenomenon understood by all the world—Russian heavy-handedness? For what reason are our hands so heavy? What weighs them down?

Another cup of coffee, another cigarette, and I'll go up on deck. The Siberian expanse, the olive-green immensity—it would frighten you, I think; but it makes Russians feel important. The mass of the land, of the country, the size of the stake in the planet: it is this that haunts us, and it is this that overthrows the sanity of the state . . . We are cruising north, but downriver. Which feels anomalous. Up on deck, it's as if the ship is motionless and the facing riverbanks are on the move. We are still; the riverbanks bob and undulate. You are borne forward by a power that is traveling the other way. You have a sense, too, that you are looming up over the shoulder of the world and heading toward an infinite waterfall. Here be monsters.

My eyes, in the Conradian sense, have stopped being Western and started being Eastern. I am back in the bosom of a vast slum family. Now it has to fend for itself. All the money has been divided up between the felons and the state.

It is curious. To type the word "Kansas" still seems reassuringly banal. And to type the word "Krasnoyarsk" still seems wholly grotesque. I could of course type "K——," like a writer from another age. "He journeyed to M——, the capital of R——." But you're a big girl now. "Moscow," "Russia": nothing you haven't seen before. My mother tongue—I find I want to use it as little as possible. If Russia is going, then Russian is already gone. We were very late, you see, to develop a language of feeling; the process was arrested after barely a century, and now all the implied associations and resonances are lost. I must just say that it does feel consistently euphemistic—telling my story in English, and in old-style English English, what's more. My story would be even worse in Russian. For it is truly a tale of gutturals and nasals and whistling sibilants.

The rest of me, even so, is becoming Eastern—re-Russifying, all over again. So keep a lookout, hereafter, for other national traits: the freedom from all responsibility and scruple, the energetic championship of views and beliefs that are not only irreconcilable but also mutually exclusive, the weakness for a humor of squalor and cynicism, the tendency to speak most passionately when being most insincere, and the thirst for abstract argument (abstract to the point of pretension) at unlikely moments—say, in the middle of a prison stampede, at the climax of a cholera riot, or in the most sepulchral phase of a terror-famine.

Oh, and just to get this out of the way. It's not the USSR I don't like. What I don't like is the northern Eurasian plain. I don't like the "directed democracy," and I don't like Soviet power, and I don't like the tsars, and I don't like the Mongol overlords, and I don't like the theocratic dynasts of old Moscow and old Kiev. I don't like the multi-ethnic, twelve-time-zone land empire. I don't like the northern Eurasian plain.

Please indulge the slight eccentricity in my use of dialogue. I'm not being Russian. I'm being "English." I feel it's bad form to quote oneself. Put it that way.

Yes, so far as the individual is concerned, Venus, it may very well be true that character is destiny. And the other way around. But on the larger scale character means nothing. On the larger scale, destiny is demographics; and demographics is a monster. When you look into it, when you look into the Russian case, you feel the stirrings of a massive force, a force not only blind but altogether insentient, like an earthquake or a tidal wave. Nothing like this has ever happened before.

17

There it is in front of me on the screen of my computer, the graph with its two crinkly lines intersecting, one pink, one blue. The birth rate, the death rate. They call it the Russian cross.

I was there when my country started to die: the night of July 31, 1956, in the House of Meetings, just above the sixty-ninth parallel.

2.
House of Meetings

It was with some ceremony, I remember, that I showed my younger brother the place where he would entertain his bride. I say "bride." They'd been married for eight years. But this would be their first night together as husband and wife . . . You head north from the zona, and after half a mile you strike off to the left and climb the steep little lane and the implausible flight of old stone steps, and there it is: beyond, on the slope of Mount Schweinsteiger, the two-story chalet called the House of Meetings, and, to the side, its envied annex, a lone log cabin like an outpost of utter freedom.

Just the one room, of course: the narrow cot with its furry undersheet and dead-weight gray blanket, the water barrel with the tin mug chained to it, the spotless slops-bucket with its tactful wooden lid. And then the chair (armless, backless), and the waiting supper tray—two fist-sized lumps of bread, a whole herring (slightly green around the edges), and the big jug of cold broth with at least four or five beads of fat set into its surface. Many hours had gone into this, and many hands.

Lev whistled.

19

I said, Well, kid, we've come a long way. Look.

"Jesus Christ," he said.

And I produced from my pocket the squat thermos of vodka, the six cigarettes (rolled out of the state newspaper), and the two candles.

Maybe he was still recovering from the power-hose and the shearer—there were droplets of sweat on his upper lip. But then he gave me the look I knew well: the mirthless rictus, with the two inverted chevrons in the middle of his brow. This I took, with considerable confidence, to be an expression of sexual doubt. Sexual doubt—the exclusively male burden. Tell me, my dear: what is it there for? The utilitarian answer, I suppose, would be that it's meant to stop us from reproducing if we're weak and sickly or just too old. Perhaps, also (this would have been at the planning stage of the masculine idea), it was felt that the occasional fiasco, or the fiasco as an ever-present possibility, might help to keep men honest. This would have been at the planning stage.

Lev, my boy? I said. You've got a goddamned paradise in here. And then I told him, with all due diffidence, not to expect too much. *She* won't. So don't you either.

He said, "I don't think I do expect too much."

We embraced. As I ducked out of the shed and straightened up, I saw something I hadn't noticed, on the windowsill—and much magnified, now, by a lenslike swelling in the glass. It was a test tube, with rounded base, kept upright by a hand-carved wooden frame. A single stemless wildflower floated in it, overflowed it—an amorous burgundy. I remember thinking that it looked like an experiment on the male idea. A poetic experiment, perhaps, but still an experiment.

The guard stepped forward and gestured with his firearm: I was to precede him down the path. Coming the other way and also under escort was my sister-in-law. That walk of hers, that famous tottering swagger—it set a world in motion.

By now the five-week Arctic summer was under way. It was as if nature woke up in July and realized how badly she had neglected her guests; and then of course she completely overdid it. There was something gushing and hysterical in the show she put on: the sun with its dial turned up, and staring, in constant attendance; the red carpet of wildflowers, the colors lush but sharply irritant, making the eyes itch; and the thrilled mosquitoes, the size of hummingbirds. I walked on, under a hairnet of midges, of gnats and no-see-ums. There was, I remember, an enormous glinting gray cloud overhead; its leading edge had a chewed look, and was about to shred or grate itself into rain.

The night of July 31, 1956: the night of crunch and crux. How did I spend it?

First, Count Krzysztov's Coffee Shop. In Count Krzysztov's Coffee Shop, this was how it went: trying not to laugh, Krzysztov served you a cup of hot black muck; and, trying not to laugh, you drank it. Krzysztov told me, inter alia, that there was going to be a lecture in the mess hall at eight o'clock—on Iran. Lectures on foreign countries, particularly contiguous foreign countries, were always very popular ("The Maoris of New Zealand" wouldn't draw much of a crowd, but anything on Finland or Mongolia would be packed). This was because a description of life across the border gave flesh to fantasies of escape. The men sat there glazedly, as if watching an exotic dancer. For analagous reasons, by far the most successful play they ever staged was a double bill, two obscure and anonymous fragments called "Three Sluggards" and "Kedril the Gorger." It was so popular that they revived it almost monthly; and Lev and I always fought our way in, along with everybody else. Ah, the cult of "Three Sluggards" and "Kedril the Gorger" . . . But it was my idea, that night, to avoid stimulation. Instead I sought a mild depressant. So I paid a call on Tanya.

Our camp had been coeducational since 1953, when the dividing wall came down, and many of us now had ladyfriends. We dreamed up a wide variety of generic names for them (as they did for us: "my heart-throb," "my sugar daddy," "my Tristan," "my Daphnis"), and you could tell a lot about a man by the way he referred to his girl. "My Eve," "my goddess," or indeed "my wife" indicated a romantic; less fastidious types used every possible synonym for copulation, plus every possible synonym for the vulva. But although there were real liaisons (pregnancies, abortions, even marriages, even divorces), ninety percent of them, I would guess, were wholly platonic. I know mine was. Tanya was a factory girl, and her crime was not political. She was a "three-timer." Three times she had done it: shown up twenty minutes late for work. Less tenderly than it may at first seem, I called her "my Dulcinea": like Quixote's mistress, she was largely a project of the imagination.

The love of one prisoner for another could be a thing of great purity. There were in fact enormous quantities of thwarted love, of trapped love, in the slave archipelago. Avowals, betrothals, hands clasped through the wire. Once, at a transit camp, I saw a spontaneous mass wedding (with priest) of scores of perfect strangers, who were then resegregated and marched off in opposite directions . . . My thing with Tanya was earthbound and workaday. I had simply discovered that having someone to look after, or look out for, shored up my will to survive. And that was all.

That night our tryst was not a success. It remained axiomatic, in camp, that the women were tougher and more durable than the men. They pitied us and mothered us. You too would have pitied us and mothered us. Our filth, our rags, our drift into hopeless self-neglect . . . They were stronger; but the price they paid was the evaporation of all their feminine essence, every last drop of their dew. "I am both a cow and a bull," wrote the encamped poetess, "A woman and a man." No, my dear, you are neither. The hormones were no longer being produced. It was the same for us. We were all heading toward neither.

Usually I could conjure with Tanya, and re-create the

little darling she must surely have been in freedom. But that night, as we sat for an hour on the tree stumps in the clearing behind the infirmary, all I could manage was a kind of callous fascination. It was her mouth. Her mouth resembled one of the etched hieroglyphs you see on the walls of the cell of the prototypical solitary, in cartoons, in the illustrations to nineteenth-century novels about epic confinements: a horizontal line measured off with six notched verticals, representing yet another week of your time. The only impulse resembling desire that Tanya awoke in me was an evanescent urge to eat her shirt buttons, which were made from pellets of chewed bread. Oh yes: and the sandpapery grain of the flushed flesh of her cheeks, in the white dusk, made me long for the rind of an orange. A week later they shipped her out. She was your age. She was twenty-four.

Midnight came and went. I turned in. When you come to camp, the seven deadly sins strike up a new configuration. Your mainstays in freedom, pride and avarice, are instantly jettisoned, to be replaced, as rampant obsessions, sparkling with unsuspected delights, by the two you never used to think about: gluttony and sloth. As my mind patrolled the House of Meetings, where Lev lay with a woman who looked like a woman, I lay alone with the other three—envy, lust, and anger.

All around me, now, was the faint but unanimous sound of slurping and rinsing. It might have seemed encouragingly lubricious if you didn't know what it was. But I knew. It was the sound of three hundred men eating in their sleep.

. . .

Life was easy, in 1956. There was the dirt and the cold, the hunger and the hate; but life was easy. Joseph Vissarionovich was dead, Beria had fallen, and Nikita Sergeyevich had made the Secret Speech.* The Secret Speech caused a planetary sensation. It was "the first time" a Russian leader had ever acknowledged the transgressions of the state. It was the first time. It was the last time too, more or less; but we'll come to that.

Joseph Vissarionovich: I knew his face better than I knew my own mother's. The mustachioed smile of a recruiting sergeant (I want *you*) and then the yellowy, grudge-hoarding, mountain-dwelling eyes, gazing from the shadows of crag or crevice.

He wants you but you don't want him. I use the "correct" form, Christian name and patronymic, Venus, to establish distance. For many years this distance did not exist. You must try hard to imagine it, the disgusting proximity of the state, its body odor, its breath on your neck, its stupidly expectant stare.

In the end it is above all embarrassing to have been so intimately shaped by such a presence. By such a sky-filler

* Joseph Vissarionovich is Stalin, leader of Russia, 1928?–53. Lavrenti Beria was head of the Cheka, or secret police, 1938–53. Nikita Sergeyevich is Khrushchev, leader of Russia, 1953–64. I see no way around these footnotes. It would have cost the memoirist his soul, I know, to write out the word *Stalin*.

and ocean-straddler as Joseph Vissarionovich. And I fought in the war he had with the other one: the one in Germany. These two leaders had certain things in common: shortness of stature, bad teeth, anti-Semitism. One had an unusually good memory; one was an hysterical but evidently compelling speaker, compelling, at any rate, to that nation at that time. And there was of course the strength of their will to power. Otherwise, they were both undistinguished men.

"I am not a character in a novel," says Conrad's Razumov, more than once (as the dreadful dilemma solidifies around him), and very reasonably, I think. I am not a character in a novel either. Like many millions of others, I and my brother are characters in a work of social history from below, in the age of the titanic nonentities.

But life was easy in 1956.

3.

The War Between the Brutes and the Bitches

My brother Lev came to Norlag in February 1948 (I was already there), at the height of the war between the brutes and the bitches. He came at night. I recognized him instantly, in a crowd and at a distance, because a sibling, Venus, far more tellingly than a child, displaces a fixed amount of air. A child grows, while its parent remains static in space. With brothers it is always the same difference.

I was having a smoke with Semyon and Johnreed on the roof of the cement works, and I saw Lev filing into the disinfection block, which stood foolishly exposed by its great battery of encaged lightbulbs. Forty minutes later he filed into the yard. He was naked but for the catsuit of thick white ointment they hosed you down with, for the purgation of small vermin; the caustic fire it generated on the surface of the skin did nothing to ease the galvanic shivering caused by thirty degrees of frost. He stumbled (he was nightblind), and went down on all fours, and the cold really took him: he looked like a hairless dog trying to shake itself dry. Then he got to his feet and stood there, holding something in his cupped hands—something precious. I kept back.

27

This was the year when the tutelary powers lost their hold on the monopoly of violence. It was a time of spasm savagery, with brute going at bitch and bitch going at brute. The factions had, at their disposal, a toolshop each, and this set the tone of their encounters: warm work with the spanner and the pliers, the handspike and the crowbar, vicings, awlings, lathings, manic jackhammerings, atrocious chiselings. Even as Lev jogged across the yard to the infirmary, there came through the mist the ear-hurting screams from the entrance to the toy factory, where two brutes (we later learned) were being castrated by a gang of bitches armed with whipsaws, in retaliation for a blinding earlier that day.

The war between the brutes and the bitches was a civil war, because the brutes and the bitches were, alike, urkas. A social substratum of hereditary criminals, the urkas had been in existence for centuries—but invisibly. They were fugitive in both senses: on the run, and quick to disappear. Outside in the land of freedom you would glimpse them rarely, and with callow wonder, as a child glimpses the half-hidden figures in the wings at a circus or a fairground: a world of Siamese twins and mermen and bearded ladies, of monstrous tattoos and scarifications, a world of coded chaos. You could *hear* them, too, sometimes: in a Moscow backstreet it could stop you dead—the urka whistle, scandalously shrill (and involving, you felt sure, indecent use of the tongue). On the outside, the urkas were a spectral underclass. In the camps, of course, they formed a conspicuous and vociferous elite. But now they were at war.

This was how power was distributed in our animal farm.

At the top were the *pigs*—the janitoriat of administrators and guards. Next came the *urkas:* designated as "socially friendly elements," they had the status of trusties who, moreover, did no work. Beneath the urkas were the *snakes*—the informers, the one-in-tens—and beneath the snakes were the *leeches*, bourgeois fraudsters (counterfeiters and embezzlers and the like). Close to the bottom of the pyramid came the *fascists*, the counters, the fifty-eighters, the enemies of the people, the politicals. Then you got the *locusts*, the juveniles, the little calibans: by-blows of revolution, displacement, and terror, they were the feral orphans of the Soviet experiment. Without their nonsensical laws and protocols, the urkas would have been just like the locusts, only bigger. The locusts had no norms at all . . . Finally, right down there in the dust were the *shiteaters*, the goners, the wicks; they couldn't work anymore, and they could no longer bear the pains of hunger, so they feebly brawled over the slops and the garbage. Like my brother, I was a "socially hostile element," a political, a fascist. Needless to say, I was not a fascist. I was a Communist. And a Communist I remained until the early afternoon of August 1, 1956. There were also animals, real animals, in our animal farm. Dogs.

The urka civil war was a consequence of Moscow's attempt to undermine urka power and urka idleness. Its policy was to promote the urkas still further: to give them, in exchange for certain duties, pay and privileges close to those of the janitoriat. The bitches were the urkas who wanted to stop being urkas and start being pigs; the brutes were the urkas who wanted to go on being urkas. It looked good for us at first, when the war broke out. Suddenly the urkas had something else to do with their inexhaustible free time—something other than torturing the fascists, their premier activity. But now the war between the brutes and the bitches was getting out of control. Having lost their monopoly of violence, the pigs applied yet more violence. There was a wildness and randomness in the air that was beginning to feel almost abstract.

Venus. Remember how disappointed you were by the crocodiles in the reptile house at the zoo—because "the lizards never moved"? Imagine that hibernatory quiet, that noisome stasis. Then comes a whiplash, a convulsion of fantastic instantaneity; and after half a second one of the crocodiles is over in the corner, rigid and half-dead with shock, and missing its upper jaw. *That* was the war between the brutes and the bitches.

Now, when I talk, here and elsewhere, of Moscow and its so-called policies, I do so with the assurance of informed hindsight. But at the time we had no idea what was going on. We never had any idea what was going on.

Lev's first day (he would spend most of it with the medics and the work-assigners) was also the monthly day of rest.

I came up behind him in the yard. He was sitting on a low stone wall where the well used to be, his knees pressed together, his shoulders sloped forward. He was cherishing his fractured spectacles, and trying to believe his eyes.

And what did he see? The thing that was hardest to grasp was the *scale*—the inordinate amount of space needed to contain it. In his line of sight were five thousand men (ten times that number lay to the sides, beyond, behind). When you got used to that, you had to come to terms with the evident fact that you were living in something like an army base, where the conscripts had been drawn from a direly indigent madhouse. Or a direly indigent hospice. In your nose and mouth was the humid breath of the camp, of Norlag, and, more distantly, the fresh cement of the brand-new Arctic city, the monumental denture of Predposylov. And finally you had to absorb and assent to the ceaseless agitation, the mad dance of the stick insects—the nervous fury of the zona.

I said, Don't turn around, Dmitriko.

Never again would I call him that. It was not the time for diminutives. It never was the time . . . A camp administrator who allowed two family members to set eyes on each other, let alone meet and talk (let alone cohabit, for almost ten years), would be punished for criminal leniency. On the other hand we would not need to be masters of deception, I didn't think, to avoid exposure. We were half-brothers with different surnames, and we were radically unalike. To be brief. My father, Valery, was a Cossack (duly de-Cossackized in 1920, when I was one). Lev's father, Dmitri, was a well-to-do peasant, or kulak (duly de-kulakized in 1932, when Lev was three). The father's genes predominated: I was six foot two, with thick black hair and orderly features, whereas Lev . . .

It seems that I had better describe him now, your step-uncle, to prepare the ground for the thunderclap that is barely a page away. There was something yokelish, indeed almost troglodytic, in the asymmetries of his face, the features thrown together inattentively, as if in the dark. Even his ears seemed to belong to two completely different people. Say whatever else you like about it, but my nose was unquestionably a nose, while Lev's was a mere protuberance. And when you looked at him side-on, you thought, Is that his chin or his Adam's apple? He was also, as a kid, short, meager, and sickly—a stuttering bedwetter in inch-thick glasses. All he had was his smile (in the mess of his face lived the teeth of a beautiful woman) and his rich blue eyes, the eyes of an *intelligent*. Definitely an *intelligent*.

I said—Don't turn around. And when you do, show no pleasure in seeing your older brother.

He stood up; he walked away, then circled back into range. For a moment I found his faintly hooded, self-caressing expression impossible to read; it seemed, in the circumstances, simply alien. After the jail and the interrogation, after the transport, many new arrivals were already mad; and I feared my brother was already mad.

"Guess what happened to me," he said.

I said, patiently, You got arrested.

"No. Well, yes. But no. I got *married*."

Congratulations, I said. So you finally knocked up little Ada. Or was it little Olga?

He didn't answer. Look at the eyes now—the eyes of an Old Believer. Part of his mind was away somewhere, dancing with itself. This was clearly a great coup of love he had brought off: a grand slam of love. Has it ever happened to you, Venus? The color of the day suddenly changes to shadow. And you know you're going to remember that moment for the rest of your life. Registering an impressive contraction of the heart, I said,

Not *Zoya*.

He nodded. "Zoya."

. . . You little *cunt*, I said. And I wheeled away from him into the yard.

After a time, as I staggered along, buckling and straightening, shaking my head, scratching my hair, I felt him settling into step beside me.

"I'm sorry. Please don't hate me. I'm so sorry."

No you're not. I turned. And with an older brother's grooved cruelty (spinning it out for at least three syllables), I said, *You?*

We sucked up breath and looked out into the sector. And saw what? In the space of three minutes we saw a bitch sprinting flat-out after a brute with a bloody mattock in his hand, a pig methodically clubbing a fascist to the ground, a workshy snake slicing off the remaining fingers of his left hand, a team of locusts twirling an old shiteater into the compost heap, and, finally, a leech who, with his teeth sticking out from his gums at right-angles (scurvy), was nonetheless making a serious attempt to eat his shoe.

I whispered it: Lev and Zoya got married. If I can survive that, then I'll never die.

"No, brother, you'll never die."

Sighing heroically, I added in a clear voice,

And *you* can survive *this*. And now you'll have to.

4.

Zoya

When a man conclusively exalts one woman, and one woman only, "above all others," you can be pretty sure you are dealing with a misogynist. It frees him up for thinking the rest are shit. So what am I? You have consumed your share of Russian novels: every time a new character appears, there is a chapter break and you are suddenly reading about his grandparents. This too is a digression. And its import is sexual. So do yourself a favor, and go and get the framed photograph on my desk and prop it up in front of you as you read. I don't want you thinking about the way I am now. I want you thinking about that twenty-five-year-old lieutenant who is throwing his hat into the air on Victory Day.

Listen. In Russia, after the war, there was a shortage of everything, including bread. There was, in fact, a famine in Russia, after the war, and two *more* million died. There was also a shortage of men. Well, there was a shortage of women too (and of children, and of old people), but the shortage of men was so extreme that Russia never recovered from it: the disparity, today, is ten million. So it was a corruptingly good time to be male in Russia, after the war, particularly if you were a handsome (and wounded) frontliner, as I was, returning to the great well of gratitude and relief, and even more particularly if, as I was, you were corrupt already. My dealings with women, I concede, were ruthless and shameless and faithless, and solipsistic to the point of malevolence. My behavior is perhaps easily explained: in the first three months of 1945, I raped my way across what would soon be East Germany.

It would suit me very well if, at this point, I could easternize your Western eyes, your Western heart. "The Russian soldiers were raping every German woman from eight to eighty," wrote one witness. "It was an army of rapists." And, yes, I marched with the rapist army. I could seek safety in numbers, and lose myself in the peer group; for we do know, Venus (the key study is *Police Battalion 101*), that middle-aged German schoolteachers, almost without exception, chose to machine-gun women and children all day rather than ask for reassignment and face the consequence. The consequence was not an official punishment, like being sent to the front, or even any mark of official disfavor; the consequence was a few days of peer displeasure before your transfer came through—the harsh words, all that jostling in the lunch queue. So you see, Venus, the peer group can make people do *anything*, and do it day in and day out. In the rapist army, everybody raped. Even the colonels raped. And I raped too.

There is a further mitigating circumstance: namely the Second World War, and four years on the dirtiest front of the dirtiest fight in history. Don't apply zero tolerance—a policy that calls for zero thought. I ask you not to turn your face away. I paid a price, as I said, and I have work, specific work, ahead of me to pay it fully. I have work to do and I will do it. I know I will. So Venus, I ask you to read on, merely noting, for now, the formation of a certain kind of masculine nature. A bashful and bookish youth, finding his feet in the 1930s (a time of catastrophe and pan-terror but also, if you please, a time of watchful prudishness from above), I lost my virginity to a Silesian housewife, in a roadside ditch, after a ten-minute chase. No. It was not the most auspicious of awakenings. I will add, in a pedagogic spirit, that the weaponization of the phallus, in victory, is an ancient fact, and one we saw remanifested on a vast scale, in Europe, in 1999. On my front, in 1945, many, many women were murdered as well as raped. I did no killing of women. Not then.

I am about to describe an unusually attractive young girl, and experience tells me that you won't like it, because that's what you are too. I'm sure you think you've evolved out of it—out of invidiousness; but evolution is not the work of an afternoon. And in my experience an attractive woman doesn't want to hear about some *other* attractive woman. It is the more problematic, perhaps, in that you will feel a protective pang for your mother, as is only right. So I invite you to put yourself in the place of one of Zoya's female contemporaries. She was nineteen, and, from the outset, her reputation was frankly terrible. You will perk up at that. And yet the other girls took an exceptionalist view of Zoya. They instinctively indulged her, as a vanguard figure—*l'esprit fort*. She lived more than they did, but she also suffered more than they did; and she showed them possibilities.

It used to be said that Moscow was the biggest village in Russia. On the outskirts, in winter, there were little paths connecting each house with tram stops and food stores (Milk, said the sign), and everyone shuffled around like rustics in their short sheepskin coats, and you expected mammoths and icebergs. But that's a memory from childhood (no milk today). It changed: a primitive entanglement in which various foundries and blast furnaces and gasworks and tanneries had been planked down among the cottages and cobblestones. We had a village within the village (the district in the southeast known as the Elbow), and when Zoya walked into it, in January 1946, she was like a rebuke to the prevailing conditions, the absence of food and fuel, the absence of books, clothes, glass, lightbulbs, candles, matches, paper, rubber, toothpaste, string, salt, soap. No, more: she was like an act of civil disobedience. She was recklessly conspicuous, Zoya, and Jewish—a natural target for denunciation and arrest. Because that's how resentments and jealousies were resolved in my country, for hundreds of years. That's how a "love triangle" could be wonderfully simplified. An anonymous phone call, or an unsigned letter, to the secret police. You kept expecting it, but there she was, every day, not in camp or in prison but on the street, with the same smile, the same walk.

And I surprised myself: I, the heroic rapist, with the

medals and the yellow badge. My first thought was not the first thought I was used to—some variant of *When can I wrench her clothes off?* No. It was this (and the sentence came to me unbidden and fully formed): *How many poets are going to kill themselves because of you?* Zoya was not an acquired taste. Her face was original (more Turkic than Jewish, the nose pointing down, not out, the mouth improbably broad whenever she laughed or wept), but her figure was a platitude—tall and ample and also wasp-waisted. Every male was condemned to receive its message. You felt it down the length of your spine. We all got it, from the street draggletail who pleaded to carry her books and hold her hand, right the way up to our pale and ancient postman who, each morning, stopped and stared at her with his mouth unevenly agape and one eye shut, as if over a gunsight.

Perhaps the single most unbelievably wonderful thing about her was that she had her own place: an attic the size of a parking bay, two floors up from her grandmother, but with its own stairs and its own front door. A nineteen-year-old girl, in Moscow, who had her own room: the equivalent, Venus, in Chicago, would be a nineteen-year-old girl who had her own yacht. You could see her going in there at night, with a man; you could see her coming out of there, with a man, *in the morning*. And there was something else. You won't believe this, but under the circumstances I can't omit it. One of the more malarial rumors attached to her was that, before each liaison, she went through some kind of Hasidic ablution that guarded her from pregnancy. This, then, was her preferred approach to the Jewish business of killing Christian babies. There were of course no contraceptives in Russia in 1946; and, as your prospective lovers monotonously reminded you, the penalty for abortion (quite mild, considering) was two years in jail.

We know quite a lot about the consequences of rape—for the raped. Understandably little sleep has been lost over the consequences of rape for the rapist. The peculiar resonance of his postcoital tristesse, for example; no animal is ever sadder than the rapist . . . As for the longer-term effects, what they were for me I now came to understand. This was the mental form they took: I couldn't see women whole, intact and entire. I couldn't even see their bodies whole. Now, Zoya wielded an outrageous allocation of physical gifts, and it would have been my style to atomize them: to do what Marvell did to the coy mistress (even her breasts, remember, were to be considered separately), to carve her up on the marble slab, each bit pierced by a flag-pin, and bearing a price. That's the way my mind went at it. So, to encapsulate: Zoya, unlike "all the others," I saw as indivisible. Being indivisible was her prime constituent. Each action involved the whole of her. When she walked, everything swayed. When she laughed, everything shook. When she sneezed—you felt that absolutely anything might happen. And when she talked, when she argued and opposed, across a tabletop, she leaned into it and performed a sedentary belly dance of rebuttal. And naturally I wondered what else she did like that, with the whole of her body. We were neighbors, and also colleagues at the Tech, the Institute for Systems, where she studied in the Jewish stream. I was twenty-five and she was nineteen. And Lev, for Christ's sake, was still at school.

She used to run a regular errand for her mother, old Ester, bringing a few edible odds and ends for the scrofulous rabbi who lay endlessly praying and dying in the basement beneath our flat. The only way to get there was through the ground floor and down the spiral staircase outside our kitchen. These iron steps were often sheathed in ice, and after a mishap or two she reluctantly fell in with my soldierly insistence that I should lead her there by the hand. She was actually not at all steady on her feet, and she knew it; much later, Lev would learn that she lacked certain spatial wirings, certain readinesses, because, as a child, she had never learned how to crawl . . . At the door to the basement she would always give me a smile of gratitude, and I always wondered what the force was, the force preventing me from throwing my arms around her, or even meeting her eye, but the force was there, and it was a strong force. "Call my name when you want to come back," I said. But she never did. From the look of her, sometimes, I thought she scaled those steps on her hands and knees. Then one night I heard her voice, lost and hoarse, calling my name. I went out and took her surprisingly warm hand in mine.

Jesus, I said at the top. I thought *I* was going to take a toss.

She smiled greedily and said, "You'd have to be a bloody mountain goat to get up there."

We laughed. And I was lost.

Yes, Venus, at that point my desperate fascination became fulminant love; and it came on me like an honor. I had all the troubadour symptoms: not eating, not sleeping, and sighing with every other breath. Do you remember Montague, the father, in *Romeo and Juliet*—"Away from light steals home my heavy son"? That's what I was, heavy, incredibly heavy. It is the heaviness you feel when, after an hour-long fight for your life in an anarchic sea, you come out of the surf, drop to the sand, and feel the massive pull of the center of the earth. Every morning I would wonder how the bed could bear my weight. I wrote poems. I walked out at night. I liked standing in the shadows across the street from her house, in the rain, in the sleet, or (this was best) in an electric storm. When the blind was up you knew that you would still be there to watch her close it.

I once saw a man leaning against the window frame, his armpits insolently singleted, his chin upraised. I was jealous, and all that, but I was also sharply aroused. That's right. I could sulk and pine, but my obsession was dependably and gothically carnal. I further confess that, while not really believing it, I was much taken with the story about the prophylactic ablution. I was used to a certain pattern—half-clothed fumblings, messy intercrural compromises, and snuffling aftermaths; and this would be happening on stairwells, in alleys and bombsites—or on a carpet or against a table, with an extended family heaped up on the other side of a locked door. Oral "relief," lasting half a minute, was the sex act of choice and necessity. And I offer this final observation (very vulgar, but not entirely gratuitous) in a pedagogic spirit, because it shows that even in their most intimate dealings the women, too, were worked on by socioeconomic reality. In the postwar years, there were no non-swallowers in the Soviet Union. None.

Absent that little flourish of enthusiasm, and the sexual atmosphere was one of coercion: my humorless insistence, their faltering submission. So in Zoya's turret, under its witchy, candlesnuffer apex, there awaited something more futuristic than female consent or even female abandonment. I mean female lust.

"Do you know what you look like when you're with her?"

Lev said this, I thought, with dissimulated ill will: I had just declined his offer of a game of chess with an abstracted, frivolity-imputing wave of the hand. So I readied myself.

"I'll tell you what you look like. If you want."

He was more advanced, and much busier, than I was, at seventeen, in the matter of girls. And so were his friends. In addition, the shortage of housing was slightly eased by the shortage of people; there was just a little more space and air—though I was never sure how far Lev got, in those secluded intervals, with his various Adas and Olgas . . . The tempo of the age was speeding up, or was trying to. You can't see yourself in history, but that's where you are, in history; and, after World War I, revolution, terror, famine, civil war, terror-famine, more terror, World War II, and more famine, there was a feeling that things could not but change. Universal dissatisfaction took the following form: everyone everywhere complained about everything. We all sensed that reality would change. But the state sensed our sensing it, and reality would not change.

All right, I said. What do I look like?

He had a certain expression, sometimes, that I knew, that I feared—a sharpened focus, an amusement with something savage in it.

"You look like Vronsky when he starts shadowing Anna. 'Like an intelligent dog that knows it's done wrong.'"

I transcribe Lev's speech in the normal way, but in fact he spoke with a stutter. And a stutter is something that prose cannot duplicate. To write "d-d-d-dog" is perfunctory to the point of insult. And *stuttering* is in any case a poor word for what used to happen to Lev. It was more like a sudden inability to speak—or even to breathe. First, the tensing, the momentary glint of self-hatred, then the little nose went up and the fight began. My brother looked far from his best at such moments, with his head stretched back and his nostrils staring at you like a pair of importunate eyes. When people stutter, you just sit through it and watch. You can't just turn away. And, with Lev, I always wanted to know what he was going to say. Even when he was a child, before the stutter came, I always wanted to know what he was going to say.

"Yes, I'm afraid so," he said, poking out his cigarette. "And anyway. She's already got a boyfriend."

I said, I know she has. And I'm waiting him out.

"... Yup, that's it," he concluded with satisfaction (as if dusting his palms). "That's what you look like. You look like a clever dog that knows it's about to be thrashed."

My brother started smoking early. He started drinking early too, and having girlfriends early. Increasingly, people do everything early in Russia. Because there isn't much time.

5.

Among the Shiteaters

People always talked about the strange light in a shiteater's eyes—that shiteater glitter. It disturbed me very much when I identified the strange light as flirtatious and peculiarly feminine. Like the moist brightness in the eye of an unpredictable aunt who has drunk too much at Easter, and is about to obey an impulse she knows to be ill-advised—a kiss, a squeeze, a pinch . . . Furtive yet conspiratorial, that shiteater glitter had something to say and something to ask. I have crossed a line, it said. And it asked: Why don't you cross it too?

We stood among them, the shiteaters, Lev and I, outside the bolted door of the kitchens, in darkness and fine rain. The fine rain, not even falling, but floating, like the gnats and midges of July. He was coming to the end of his first day, and I had chosen this place for a conversation we very much needed to have. The shiteaters loomed and swayed beneath the lone lightbulb, waiting for the last buckets to be tipped out of the back window. By now the pigs seldom came by, seldom bothered them, because no amount of beating could keep a shiteater from the slops. There seemed to be very little physical pain—where they lived, beyond the line they had crossed.

Even within the stratum of the shiteaters, Venus, there were two echelons. There were some shiteaters that the other shiteaters looked down on. These were known as *all-fours shiteaters* . . . I relay these details, my dear, these details of awlings and chiselings, of educated, even cultivated men eating slops on their hands and knees, because I want you to think about their *strangeness*. Wildly directed violence, drastic degradation: this is all terribly *strange*.

"Why's it so fucking *dark* around here," he said.

It was a complaint, not a question. Lev, the swot geographer, knew why it was so dark around here.

"Yes yes," he said. "This is the Arctic in February. The sun'll come up in March. What do I do, brother? What do I do?"

I was ready for this. The majority of the fascists who got ten-year sentences in 1937–38 had been rearrested, in alphabetical order, and resentenced in 1947–48. And they all looked like Lev. Older, thinner, wilder—but they all looked like Lev, the rapidly blinking *intelligent*, with his hopeless shoes (vastly dissimilar, but each a dog's dinner of frayed rope and car tire), his half a book, and his torn summer jacket. And always cherishing the fractured spectacles. Whereas the new fascists were men who had spent five years in the Red Army. For us the camp was just more war, with one startling difference. We had fought the fascists—the enemy. Then the Russian state, now fascist itself, told us that *we* were the fascists, and they were arresting us for it and enslaving us for it. Now we were the enemy, to be flung out over the shoulder of the world. I have noticed that you and your crowd have a high tolerance for self-pity in others, so I will add the following. What made this capsizal hard to forget was that my war wound throbbed in the cold from September to June. But I mustn't be self-pitying. I mustn't be the lachrymist. There are other things I mustn't be—the tough guy, the martyr. And I mustn't be indignant. Or earnest. That's less difficult. Americans are earnest, Russians, when the mood is on them, are earnest. While I prefer the droller cultures, and the wizened ironists, to be found on the northwestern fringe of the Eurasian plain.

What do you do? I began. Oh we'll come to that. But first—aren't you going to say it?

"Say what?"

You know: "There must have been a mistake." Or "If only someone would tell Joseph Vissarionovich."

". . . Why the fuck would I say that? They arrest *by quota*. They do. I bet they do."

Lev was right about that. The Terror, too, was driven by quota: this or that many people from this or that area and social group, at such and such a rate, quotas, norms, minimums.

"You know what's happened," he said. "You and I have been sold into slavery. All that fucking around with the interrogations and the confessions and the documents.

That's just the process of being sold into slavery. It sounds quite romantic, doesn't it, being sold into slavery . . ."

He looked around. No, there was nothing romantic about Norlag, about Predposylov.

"I mean, you'd expect somewhere hot. Jesus."

Lev was nineteen. And already he was seeing more than I saw (I had no head for politics, as will soon be evident). Looking back, now, I can recall my fever of fear when I realized that the younger brother saw more than the older. It happened over the chess board. I felt myself exposed to greater powers of combination, of permutation and penetration. And he always stood back from the general opinion, the general mood. Except when it happened to suit him, he never went along with anything. He always made his own calculation. He pushed out a rigid nether lip, slightly off center, lowered his gaze, and made the calculation.

And I asked him: Which prison?

"Butyrki."

Butyrki's great, isn't it.

"Great. In my cell I had three Red professors, two composers, and one poet. Oh yeah—and one informer. I was proud to be there. Butyrki's great."

Great. How did it go? Before.

"The usual thing. Called out of class at the Tech. Quite polite. Then for a couple of weeks I had to go to the Kennel every other day and eat shit."

A shiteater veered up at us from the darkness, and then stepped back with his blanketed forearm raised. I said,

What was the charge? Or didn't they give you one.

"They gave me one." He let out a soft snort and said, "Praising America."

I knew this to be a crime, sure enough, and one with several subsections. Many recently arrived fascists had committed it—Praising American Democracy or Praising American Technique or Abasement Before America. Or alternatively Abasement Before the West. Not a few of our number had now seen something of the West; and even in ruins it abased us . . . There were scores of *Americans* in Norlag, including an American *American*. Come over here to participate in the Soviet experiment, he told the CP man who issued his passport that he was fully prepared to take the big cut in his standard of living. That same day he got the *quarter*—twenty-five years.

And *were* you praising America?

"No. I was praising The Americas. I was in a queue with Kitty and I was praising The Americas."

Then we both did something we hadn't been expecting to do for some time to come: we laughed—with our vapor forming and fleeing. I understood. "The Americas" was sibling code for Zoya. And it was a *good* name for her too, because it caught her walk. The spatial relationship between the two continents, Venus, has best been evoked by the exile Nabokov: two figures on a trapeze, in the big top, one beneath the other, and just coming out of the backswing. But Zoya's walk also expressed it, embodied it, the giddy disjunction between north and south, and then the waist, as thin as Panama. Kitty was family, Lev's full sibling, like Vadim, the other one.

And was Kitty *dis*praising The Americas?

"You know. A bit. Basically Zoya makes Kitty feel like a pencil. No. Like Chile. That's what I told her. You're jealous of The Americas because she makes you feel like Chile."

I said, I thought Kitty was keen on Zoya.

"Kitty is riveted by Zoya. But she says she'll destroy me. Not on purpose. But that's what will happen in the end."

I would remember this. Right from the start I had fingered Zoya for a decimator of the poets, and a poet (Acmeist, Mandelstamian) was what Lev, at this stage, was in some sense hoping to be . . . There came a clatter from within and the sound of voices. The shiteaters looked up, with thin mouths and smiling eyes.

"Chile," Lev said suddenly. "You'd have to be an *island* to be less landlocked than Chile."

He sniffed, wiped his nose, and straightened his shoulders. His upper lip, temporarily beaklike, and his wary glance: he looked like what he was—an adolescent, fearing ridicule after a vulnerable remark . . . Lev had always been owlishly capable of getting excited by geography. I remember he once said, "The Pacific is the prince of the oceans. The Atlantic's a mere *strait* when compared to it." And he had a whole theory about the geography of Russia, how it determined both her history and her fate. Oh, Venus, what *good* boys we were, originally. I think I told you that our mother was a schoolteacher. She was in fact a completely different kind of human being: she was a headmistress. And therefore a harpy of ambition. "You are *intelligents*!" she used to shriek at us, often out of a clear blue sky. "You serve the *nation*, not the state!" And there we were, Lev and me, with our books and our thick periodicals, our basic German, English, French, our heavy chess pieces, our maps and charts.

I said, as I'd planned, You have arrived in hell. I don't have to tell you that. Here, man is wolf to man. But the funny thing is it's just like anywhere else.

"No it isn't. It isn't like anywhere else."

Yes it is. You came up under Vad, am I right?

Vad, Vadim, was Lev's twin brother (fraternal—profoundly nonidentical), a leering, sidling, scheming kid, and "*very* socialist," as our mother used to say as she fanned herself and blew the fringe off her brow. Tormenting Lev was Vad's chief hobby and project for fifteen years. I'd tell Lev, Hit back, hit back. And keep hitting back. And Lev did hit back. But always just that single flail, and then he'd curl himself up again to take his punishment. Vad, in 1948, was a military politico, junior but hyperactive, and stationed in East Germany. Incidentally, he resembled me more closely than he resembled his twin. Tacit family lore had it that Vadim, implacable even in the womb, had shouldered Lev to the side and then drained off everything good.

I said, Until the day came when you hit back and kept on hitting. What changed?

In ones and twos the shiteaters had started drifting off, back into the sector. Of those remaining, some seemed discouraged by the defection, and the aggregate loss of hope;

others freshly twinkled—dreaming of the lion's share, with Irish eyes . . .

Lev said, "I was different inside."

. . . *Shit*, I said. It's just struck me. What happened to your stutter? Where'd your stutter go?

He gave a taut nod and said, "She did that. After the first night, I woke up and it wasn't there. Can you imagine? You know what it means? It means I can't die. Not yet."

No, you can't die. Not yet.

Venus, you're probably marveling—I know I am—at my calm and helpfulness, and the superb urbanity of my fraternal exchange with the husband of the woman I loved, the husband of Zoya, healer of stutterers. The truth is that I was in shock. And not "still in shock" either: I had hardly started. I would go on being in shock for over a month, buoyed by buxom chemicals. They did me good, morally. I got a lot worse when they wore off.

I said, Here, *everyone's* Vad. Vad with a wrench and a screwdriver. And you haven't got fifteen years to adapt to it. You haven't got fifteen hours. You've got till tomorrow morning.

My breath hung in the air. Even in June your breath hung in the air as if you were smoking an enormous and fiery cigar. They went out six feet and curled back around you, these scarves of breath.

The last kitchen light went out, the last internal door slammed shut, and the last lingering shiteater wandered off crying childishly into his fists.

I said, This is what you've got to do.

"Tell me."

I told him. And then I said, You're what she's giving up her twenties for. Christ. Think of that. And when it's this cold, don't eat the snow. You'll have blood on your lips and your tongue. The snow burns.

I will now briefly describe the conclusion of my thing with Zoya. I will now briefly describe my abasement before The Americas.

On March 20, 1946, it came to pass that I was alone with her, in the conical attic, at half past one in the morning.

She hadn't actually asked me up. I'd simply attached myself to a group that was on its way to pay her a call. We were not good Communists, not anymore; but we were excellent communitarians. Community: the cardinal Russian strength, even though the state now feared it and hated it. Russians looked out for each other. Russians did do that . . . We sat around in our overcoats. There was no heat and no light. There was no food and no drink. We had, I remember, a paper bagful of a nameless orange tea, but no water. The tea turned out to be carrot peel. So we ate it. They were all younger than me; it was perhaps to be expected that I said very little. I didn't care how obvious it was, how dourly obvious—my determination to be the last to leave.

Because I now felt that I had a deadline. Zoya, that day,

had done something, said something, that could not but lead to her arrest, or so I judged. It will sound unserious to you, Venus; but it wasn't unserious. The whole Tech was talking about it. After classes Zoya showed up for the plenary session of the Komsomol, or the Communist Youth League. I remember the convocations of the Komsomol: try to imagine something halfway between a temperance meeting and a Nuremberg Rally. On her way out, Zoya said, quite audibly, that the two-hour keynote address (its full title, I remember, was "The Scum of the Anarcho-Syndicalist Deviation and the City Administration Committee Decision About the Party Meeting at the Mining Institute") had "bored her tits off." And no no no no no, you just *couldn't* say that. Doubly provocative, and she was trebly endangered—boredom and breasts and Jewishness. That night, every time I heard a car or a truck in the street, I thought, It's them. They're here.

A couple of days earlier, as I walked Zoya to Tech, a man going past on a bicycle shouted out something with the word *kike* in it. I asked her—Kike what?

"Dirty kike bedstraw," she repeated without any emphasis.

We walked on. I said, How often does it happen?

"You know what I'd like? I'd like to be vulgar in America. I'd like to be a Jew in America—all flash. How often? You might get nothing for a week. Then you get about nine in one day."

I'm sorry.

"It's not *your* fault."

55

Something strange was happening in the Soviet Union, after the war against fascism: fascism. By which I mean an abnormal emphasis on the *folk* (the Great Russians), together with an abnormal xenophobia. Pogrom was coming. So there were sensible, indeed cynical reasons for Zoya to look kindly on me. It was one thing to stage conspicuous entanglements with your fellow bohemians, and especially your fellow Jews; it was another thing to be the devoted companion of a tall and handsome war hero, with his medals and his yellow badge, denoting a serious wound. Not much fun to say, all that. But I'm telling you, my dear: this is the meaning, this is the daily and hourly import of state systems.

I sat with my back to the window and the moonbeams. The walls breathed or bristled in the dark. I reached out—a costume (velvet), ostrich feathers, a tasseled tambourine. With the light behind me I could stare at Zoya, seeing her singly, entire, with unprecedented indifference to detail. And I was in any case full of emotion. Untypically, for a Russian, I had been raised by my mother to regard anti-Semitism as a reflex of the gutter; and the shame I felt for my nation was so intense that it had already ruined my memory of the war. At the same time I was lost in admiration for her—for the way she hadn't flinched in the street and her resilience, now, when everyone else was mentally packing her pillowslip. You have a consciousness of this laid down in you, Venus, and I don't: how it feels to be the other. And we know, from the memoirists, about the pain, the physical pain, of wearing the star, also yellow, the burning crysanthemum of the star. You in your flesh have worn the star . . . Half of Soviet Jewry had been killed by the Germans. And now the Russians had begun to glare at the half that remained. It was coming from above but also coming from below, coming up from the depths.

At the door Zoya was saying goodnight to her penultimate guest (her farewells punctuated by a violent yawn). All the time I kept asking myself how it happened—how had I stood by and given someone such power to hurt me? In my mouth, not the usual slow drool but a humble aridity—the aching throat of the lovelorn. I would act, though, I would act; and Russia would help me. You see, when the depths stir like this, when a country sets a course for darkness, it comes to you not as horror but as unreality. Reality weighs nothing, and everything is allowed. I rose. I rose, and impended.

She placed a palm on my chest, to establish a distance, but she accepted the kiss, or withstood it; and yet, as she withdrew her mouth, she retained my lower lip for a second between her teeth, and her eyes moved sideways, ruminatively; she was chewing it over—but not at length. I said three words and she said three words. Hers were, "You frighten me . . ." A novelettish incitement, you may think. And I would once have taken it as that. But I deeply knew that she hadn't liked the taste of my lips.

"I'm sorry."

For several seconds I stood there with my hands writhing around in one another's grasp. And then I, the decorated rapist, I, who went through a woman a week using every form of flattery, false promises, bribery, and blackmail, not to mention the frank application of masculine bulk—I gave out a noise like the muffled coo of a pigeon, kissed her palm, and staggered out, seeming to twirl end over end all the way down the stairs.

They didn't come for her, of course. They came for me. And understand that it didn't feel like the worst thing that had ever happened when, ten weeks later, they gave me ten years.

This was his first morning and he was out there in the sector.

This was what I told him, as we stood among the shiteaters and their eager swirls of breath, their laughing eyes. I told him he would join their number unless he could find some murder in his heart. I told him that the acceptance of murder was the thing that was being asked of him.

This was Lev in the yard. His face, already brick-red, wore a gashed forehead and a split lip. During the bungled headcount (and recount, and re-recount), many of the men in his brigade—a strong brigade—were running on the spot, or at least flapping their arms about. Lev was doing jumping jacks.

PART II

1.

Dudinka, September 2, 2004

The phrase "dirty old man" has two meanings, and one of them happens to be literal. There is a dirty old man on board who is that kind of dirty old man. He may be a dirty old man of the other kind too, but something tells me that the two callings are difficult to combine. Now tell me, Venus. Why do I feel tempted to take the road of this dirty old man? I hate washing more and more every day, and shaving, and I hate stuffing my laundry into plastic bags and writing "socks—4 prs." I almost burst into tears, the other morning, when I realized I'd have to cut my toenails *one more time*. A really dirty old man wouldn't bother. What clarity and intrepidity, what boldness and pride. I find I deeply admire this dirty old man. His leftover-infested beard, his death-ray breath, and his rotting, many-layered overcoat are things that everyone *else* has to worry about. The smell that follows him about, and precedes him, is light-speed: you know it the instant he enters the dining room even when he's forty feet away. He behaves as though it isn't his fault and he's innocent. He's clean: in some mysterious way, he's clean. Yesterday he disembarked; I saw him, quite a distance off, being canoed through the mist—a mist perhaps of his own making—to what looked like a fish cannery lurking under the eaves of the western bank.

Women don't mind it, because baths and showers are, at least, "lovely and warm" (this was the phrase used by an English ladyfriend of mine, whom you'll meet); and it's interesting, the female admiration for warmth, combined with the well-attested tolerance of cold. But the male, I think, is eventually bored to the point of dementia by the business of not being dirty. On the other hand, I do see that it's necessary, and that it gets more necessary every day. The "high" eighties: that too has unfortunate connotations. High, late—it doesn't matter. Eighty-six is never going to sound any good.

I realize you must be jerking back from the page about three times per paragraph. And it isn't just the unvarying morbidity of my theme, and my generally poor performance, which is due to deteriorate still further. No, I mean my readiness to assert and conclude—my appetite for generalizations. Your crowd, they're so terrorstricken by generalizations that they can't even manage a declarative sentence. "I went to the store? To buy orange juice?" That's right, keep it tentative—even though it's already happened. Similarly, you say "okay" when an older hand would say (if anything), "I see" or "Oh really." "My name is Pete?" "Okay." "I was born in Ohio?" "Okay." What you're saying, with your okays, is this: for the time being I take no exception. You have not affronted me *yet*. No one has been humiliated *so far*.

A generalization might sound like an attempt to stereotype—and we can't have that. I'm at the other end. I worship generalizations. And the more sweeping the better. I am ready to kill for sweeping generalizations.

The name of your ideology, in case anyone asks, is Westernism. It would be no use to you here.

Now, at noon, the passengers and crew of the *Georgi Zhukov* are disembarking in Dudinka with as much triumphalism as their numbers will allow. The tannoy erupts, and my hangover and I edge down the gangway to the humphing and oomphing of a military march. And that's what a port looks like—a mad brass band, with its funnels and curved spouts, its hooters and foghorns, and in the middle distance the kettledrums of the storage vats.

But this is different. It is a Mars of rust, in various hues and concentrations. Some of the surfaces have dimmed to a modest apricot, losing their barnacles and asperities. Elsewhere, it looks like arterial blood, newly shed, newly dried. The rust boils and bristles, and the keel of the upended ferryboat glares out across the water with personalized fury, as if oxidation were a crime it would lay at your door.

Tottering and swaying over my cane, I think of those more or less ridiculous words, Greek-derived, for irrational fears, many of which describe more or less ridiculous conditions: anthophobia (fear of flowers), pogonophobia (beards), deipnophobia (dinner parties), triskaidekaphobia (the number thirteen). Yes, these are sensitive souls. But there's one for rust (iophobia); and I think I've got it. I've got iophobia. The condition doesn't strike me, now, as at all ridiculous—or at all irrational. Rust is the failure of the work of man. The project, the venture, the experiment: failed, given up on, and not cleaned up after.

A stupor of self-satisfaction: *that's* the state to be in when your life is drawing to an end. And not this state—not my state. It isn't death that seems so very frightening. What frightens me is life, my own, and what it's going to turn out to add up to.

There is a letter in my pocket that I have yet to read.

The big wrongs—you reach a point where you've just about bedded them down. And then the little wrongs wake up and bite, with their mean little teeth.

What's annoying me now is the state-driven prudery of the 1930s. These were my teenage years, and I might have got off to a much better start. I fondly see myself kiting with Katya, mushrooming with Masha, bobsleighing with Bronislava—first kiss, first love. But the state wouldn't have it. "Free love" was officially classified as a bourgeois deformity. It was the "free" bit they really didn't like. Still, they didn't like love either.

Only this year has it emerged—some sort of picture of the sexual mores at the court of Joseph Vissarionovich. And it unsurprisingly transpires that the revolutionary energy had its erotic aspect. The Kremlin circle, in short, was a hive of adultery and seigneurism.

It was like food and space to breathe. They could have it. And we couldn't. Why not? Sex isn't a finite resource; and free love costs nothing. Yet the state, as I think Nikita Sergeyevich pointed out, wanted to give the impression that Russia was a stranger to carnal knowledge. As you might put it—What's *that* about?

On the quay a small fleet of minivans stands by for those passengers who are impatient to reach Predposylov. No, we are not many, we are pitifully few. The Gulag tour, the purser told me with an indulgent shrug, always lost money; and then he mimed a yawn. Similarly, on the flight from the capital to my point of embarkation, I quite clearly heard a stewardess refer to me (she and a colleague were remixing my drink) as "the Gulag bore in 2B." It is nice to know that this insouciance about Russian slavery—abolished, it is true, as long ago as 1987—has filtered down to the caste of tourism. I let the stewardess get away with it. Start a ruckus on a plane these days and you get fifteen bullets in the head. But the indulgent purser (much shaken, much enriched) now knows that here is one who still swears and weeps, that here is one who still hates and burns.

We say our goodbyes, and I am alone on the quayside. I want to get to the Arctic city the way I did the first time, and I'm taking the train. After ten or fifteen minutes, and after some cursing (but no haggling), a reasonably sober longshoreman agrees to drive me to the station in his truck. What is the matter with me—why all this swearing and tipping? It could be that my behavior is intended as exemplary. I frequently transgress, it's true; but I at least am prompt with my reparations, my apologies in the form of cash.

The uncertain Arctic light, I realize, makes my body clock run too fast or too slow; every day I feel as if I have risen in the small hours or else shamefully overslept. The colors of the cars don't look quite right either, like car colors everywhere but seen at dawn under streetlamps. My hangover has not gone away. All the buildings, all the medium-rise flat blocks, stand on stout little stilts, pilings driven down through the melting permafrost and into the bedrock. This is the world of the crawlspace.

Lev's geographical theory of Russian destiny was not his alone, and serious historians now propound it. The northern Eurasian plain, with its extreme temperatures, its ungenerous soil, its remoteness from the southerly trade routes, its lack of any ocean but the Arctic; and then the Russian state, with its compulsive and self-protective expansion, its land empire of twenty nations, its continent-sized borders: all this demands a heavily authoritarian center, a vast and vigilant bureaucracy—or else Russia flies apart.

Our galaxy, too, would fly apart, if not for the massive

black holes in its core, each the size of the solar system, and the presence all around of dark matter and dark energy, policing the pull to the center.

This explanation appealed to my brother because, he said, it was "the right size": the same size as the landmass. We can shake our heads and say physics did it. Geography did it.

With its light-blue plaster and creamy trim, the railway station has the appearance of a summer pavilion, yet the bar, where I wait, is darkly congested (with locals, not travelers), and this reassures me. Until now the human sparsity of Dudinka has given me the feeling of free fall or imminent levitation. And the memories of my first journey here, in 1946, are like an awful dream of human constriction, of inconceivable crowding and milling and huddling.

A liter of hundred-proof North Korean vodka, I notice, costs less than a liter of watery Russian beer. There is also an impressive dedication, on the part of the customers, to oloroso, or fortified wine ("sweet sack"). Oloroso is a drunkard's drink as it is, and this stuff doesn't come from Jerez. That's the distinction Dostoevsky is making when he includes, on a tabletop already inauspiciously burdened with alcohol, "a bottle of the strongest sherry from the national cellar."

My hangover continues to deteriorate. Or should I say that my hangover continues to thrive? For indeed it comes on wonderfully well. I want a lot of it, I need a lot of it, but I haven't been *drunk* for fifteen years. Remember? I was lying in bed, on a Sunday afternoon, and quietly dying. Occasionally I whispered *water*—in Russian. A sign of truly bestial need. You walked in on stiffened legs, head down, intensely concentrated: you weren't going to spill the clear liquid in the pint glass you held in both hands. "Here," you said. I reached out a withered arm. And then: "It's *vodka*." And I absorbed the vicious intelligence of your stare. By then I was married to your mother. You were nine.

On the television, which perches high on the wall, there now appears the familiar and dreadful sight of the E-shaped redbrick building. I move closer, in time to hear yet another untruth: that there are "no plans" to storm the school. Then, suddenly and with no explanation, the screen fizzes, and Middle School Number One is replaced by a Latin soap opera in medias res—and, as always, under an inch of makeup each, a tearful old vamp is reproaching a haughty gigolo. The disruption goes unnoticed or at least unremarked. My instinct is to throw another costly tantrum—but directed at whom, and to what end? In any event I cannot bear it, so I pay, and tip, and wheel my case out onto the platform, and stare at the rails, narrow-gauged, that lead to the Arctic city.

No, young lady, I haven't turned my phone off. I've just been using it a lot—Middle School Number One, in North Ossetia. I was, as you know, a tolerably big cheese in Russia by the time I left, and I had many contacts in the military. You may also remember the not very serious trouble this put me to right up until 1991, when the certificate, framed in Paris, pronounced the death of the Russian experiment. Of that particular Russian experiment. My contemporaries are of course all long gone, and in many cases I deal with the sons of the men I knew. They talk to me. And I am hearing some extraordinary things.

By now the children are in their underwear and sitting with parents and teachers on the floor of the boobytrapped gymnasium. Mines clad in metal bolts are strung up on the basketball hoops. When the children chant for water they are silenced by a bullet fired into the ceiling. To aid ventilation, some of the gym windows have been obligingly shattered, but the killers, it seems, remain committed to the dehydration of their hostages, if hostages they are, and have clubbed off the tap handles in the kitchens and bathrooms. The children are now reduced, and some are now forced, to drink sweat and urine filtered through layers of clothing. How long can a child survive in great heat without water? Three days? Of *course* there are plans to storm the school.

It will be revealed, postmortem, that the killers are on heroin and morphine, and some of the doses will be described as "beyond lethal." As the power of the analgesic fades, what was numb will become raw; I keep thinking of the killer with red hair and how his rusty beard will itch and smart. Pogonophobia . . . North Ossetia has started to remind me of another school massacre, swaggering, drug-fueled—Columbine. Yes I know. Columbine was not political but purely recreational, and was over in minutes. Only the briefest visit, on that occasion, to the parallel universe where murdering the young is accounted witty.

They are now saying that the killers, who have made "no demands," are jihadis from Saudi Arábia and Yemen. Jihadis they may well be, but they are almost certainly from Chechnya, and what they want is independence. The reason that can't happen, Venus, is that Chechnya, after centuries of Russian invasion, oppression, mass deportation, and (most recently) blitz, is now organically insane. So the leader's in a bind, now, just as Joseph Vissarionovich felt himself to be with the Jews in 1948: "I can't swallow them, and I can't spit them out." All he could do was chew.

Early on in the siege of the Moscow theater—Dubrovka—in 2002, the killers released some of the children. In North Ossetia you feel that, if anyone is going to be released, it will be the adults. And we remember how Dubrovka ended. With the best will in the world, the secret police did something that might have won greater obloquy elsewhere—in Kurdistan, for example. They gassed their own civilians.* You were appalled, I remember, as were all Westerners; but here it was considered a broad success. Sitting at the breakfast table in Chicago, de-Russified and

* Immobilized by an "anesthetic aerosol," all thirty-five hostage-takers were executed in situ. Of the seven hundred hostages, one hundred and thirty were fatally gassed.

Anglophone and reading *The New York Times*, even I found myself murmuring, Mm. Not bad.

Of course there are plans to storm the school. To say *plans* risks extravagance, perhaps, but somehow or other the school will be stormed. This we know, because the Spetsnaz, our elite special forces, are buying bullets from the locals, who are surging around outside with their muskets and flintlocks.

Your peers, your equals, your secret sharers, in the West: the one Russian writer who still speaks to them is Dostoevsky, that old gasbag, jailbird, and genius. You lot all love him because his characters are fucked-up *on purpose*. This, in the end, was what Conrad couldn't stand about old Dusty and his holy fools, his penniless toffs and famished students and paranoid bureaucrats. As if life isn't hard enough, they devote themselves to the invention of pain.

And life isn't hard enough, not for you . . . I'm thinking of your first wave of boyfriends—eight or nine years ago. The shat-myself look they all favored, with the loose jeans sagging off the rump; and the eviscerated trainers. That's a prison style: no belt or laces—lest you hang yourself with them. Looking at those boys, with their sheared heads, their notched noses and scarified ears, I felt myself back in Norlag. Is this the invention of pain? Or a little reenactment of the pains of the past? The past has a weight. And the past is heavy.

I'm not for a moment saying that your anorexia was in any sense *voulu*. The force of the thing took all my courage from me, and your mother and I sobbed when we saw the CCTV tape of your dark form, like a knobbly walking stick, doing push-ups beside your hospital bed in the middle of the night. I will just add that when you went to the other place, the one called the Manor, and I saw a hundred of you through the wire around the car park, it was impossible not to think of another iconic twentieth-century scene.

Forgive me. And anyway it's not just the young. There is a Western phenomenon called the male midlife crisis. Very often it is heralded by divorce. What history might have done to you, you bring about on purpose: separation from woman and child. Don't tell me that such men aren't tasting the ancient flavors of death and defeat.

In America, with divorce achieved, the midlifer can expect to be more recreational, more discretionary. He can almost design the sort of crisis he is going to have: motorbike, teenage girlfriend, vegetarianism, jogging, sports car, mature boyfriend, cocaine, crash diet, powerboat, new baby, religion, hair transplant.

Over here, now, there's no angling around for your male midlife crisis. It is brought to you and it is always the same thing. It is death.

The train rocks and knocks across the simplified landforms of the tundra: Russia's great white page, awaiting the characters and sentences of history. No hills and valleys, just bumps and dips. Here, topographical variation is the work of man: gigantic gougings and scourings, and pyramids of slag. If you saw a mountain, now, a plateau, a cliff, it would loom like a planet. There is a hollow hill in Predposylov that is called a mountain, Mount Schweinsteiger, named after the geologist (a Russian-German, I think, from the Volga basin) who discovered nickel here toward the end of the nineteenth century. In the plains of limbless trees stand pylons, attached to no cable.

Our little train is a local, a dutiful ferrier of souls, taking them from the dormitory towns and delivering them to the Kombinat. There are some very worn faces among the passengers, and some very new ones too (shorn pinheads attached to strapping tracksuits), but they all wear masks of dormitory calm, not aware of anything unusual, not aware of anything nightmarish and unforgettable.

So in this journey am I, as the phrases go, retracing my steps—in an attempt to bring it all back? To do that, I would have needed to descend below the waterline of the *Georgi Zhukov*, and induce the passengers and crew to coat themselves in shit and sick and then lie on top of me for a month and a half. Similarly, this train, its windows barred, its carriages subdivided into wire cages, the living and the dead all bolt upright, would have to be shunted into a siding and abandoned till mid-November. And there aren't enough people—there just aren't enough people.

With an hour to go, the train makes a stop at a humble

township called Coercion. It says it on the platform: Coercion. How to explain this onset of candor? Where are the sister settlements of Fabulation and Amnesia? As we pull out of Coercion, the carriage is suddenly visited by a cloudburst of mosquitoes, and in silent unanimity—with no words or smiles or glances, with no sense of common purpose—the passengers set about killing every last one of them.

By the time they're all dead (clapped in the hands, smeared across the window), you can see it on the shallow horizon: the heavy haze, like a fleece going yellow at the edges, there to warm the impossible city.

2.

"Oh, I Can Bear It"

I told Lev, more than once, that his chances of survival were reasonably good. That was a guess. Now we can do the math.

In the Gulag, it was not the case that people died like flies. Rather, flies died like people. Or so it was said in the years before the war, when the camps were lethalized as part of the push of the Terror. There were fluctuations, but in general the death rate was determined by the availability of food. Massively and shamingly, the camp system was a phenomenon of food.

In "hungry '33" one out of seven died, in 1943 one out of five, in 1942 one out of four. By 1948 it had gone back down again, systemwide, and your chances were not much worse than in the rough-and-ready Soviet Union, or "the big zona," as it was universally known in camp: the twelve-time-zone zona. By 1948, flies had stopped dying like people, and people had gone back to dying like flies.

Still, this was the Arctic. And there was the question of his physical mass. What the body is doing, in camp, is slowly eating itself; my brother was thicker now in the chest and shoulders, but at five foot three he remained a lenten meal.

An actuary might put it this way: if there were ten Levs in Norlag, in 1948, then one of them was going to die. That still didn't mean that he had a good chance of surviving his ten-year sentence. It meant that he had a good chance of surviving 1948. Do the math, and his prospects were exactly zero. No, less than zero. Because it transpired, Venus, toward the end of the first week, that my brother wasn't merely a fascist. He was also a pacifist.

I cannot give here a full inventory of Lev's troubles, during his naturalization, and, to the extent that I do, it is because everything that happened to him in Norlag came together and converged on the night of July 31, 1956, in the House of Meetings. This was his Russian cross. And it was also mine.

For the crucial first day of general work Lev was assigned to "land clearance," and with a strong brigade. Which meant that he was lowered into a pit at six in the morning, equipped with half a shovel, and hoisted out again twelve hours later. The team got back to the sector just before eight. I scanned their faces; I stared so hard that I felt my eyes might have the power to carve him out of the air. Yes—he was among them. With dropped head, and shoulderless and bowlegged; but he was among them. I knew then that Lev had made the norm. If he hadn't, they would have left him down there until he had. The team leader, the Latvian, Markargan, would have seen to that. This was a strong brigade.

Toward the end of the week his face wasn't brick-red any more. It was black-and-blue.

You're a *what*? I said.

"A pacifist. I didn't want to tell you on the first night." He spat, bloodily, and wiped his pulped lips. "Nonviolence—that's my ticket."

Who did your face?

"There's a Tartar who covets my shovel. He's got the other half of it. I won't fight but I won't give it up. He's getting the idea. Yesterday he practically bit my hand off at the wrist—look. I'm nineteen. It'll heal. And I didn't give it up."

What is all this? I said. You can fight. I've seen you. You were even quite talented for a while—quite savory—after you did Vad. And you're stronger now. They had you digging fucking ditches in the street for four years. You're no milksop.

"I'm not weak anymore. But I'm a pacifist. I turn the other cheek. Listen," he said. "I'm not Gandhi—I don't believe in heaven. If my life is threatened, I'll fight to defend it. And I think I'd fight to defend yours. I wouldn't be able to help myself. But that's all. I have my reasons. I have my reason." He shook his head, and again he spat. "I didn't tell you this either. They killed Solomon Mikhoels."

Solomon Mikhoels was the most famous Jew in Russia: venerable actor, and intercontinental envoy. During the war he mobilized American Jewry and raised millions of dollars. Once he performed for Joseph Vissarionovich in the Kremlin. Shakespeare. *Lear*.

"The Organs killed him. 'Road accident.' They beat him to death and then a truck ran him over. It's starting. Zoya threw up when she heard."

I said, There's nothing you can do about that. What's the Tartar's name? You're not there. You're here.

"That's right. I'm here."

You see, Lev had just told me that after a week in his barracks—one of the most caked and clotted in the whole of Norlag—he was still sleeping on the floor. I feel the need for italicization: *on the floor*. And you just couldn't do that. Down there you churned in a heap of spongy shiteaters, decrepit fascists, and (another subsection) Old Believers inching their way into martyrdom. And the smell, the smell . . . As the dark-age Mongol horde approached your city, it hurt the ears when it was still some distance from the walls. More terrifying than the noise was the smell, expressly cultivated—the militarization of dirt, of heads of hair, armpits, docks, feet. And the breath: the breath, further enriched by the Mongol diet of fermented mare's milk, horse blood, and other Mongols. So it was in camp, too. The smell was penal, weaponized. The floor of the barracks was where it gathered—all the breath of the zona.

"Everything comes down on you," he conceded. "I reach into my shirt for a handful of lice. And if they're only little ones I think fuck it and put them back."

There were about fifteen reasons why he couldn't stay down there. He had to make it to the second tier. The topmost boards were, of course, the inalienable roosts of the urkas, of the brutes, of the bitches; but Lev had to make it to the second tier.

So I went through it all again, in soft-voiced earnest. Markargan will be behind you, I told him. He needs your labor—he needs your sleep, your health. You're not going to last in that brigade so use the clout *now*. Gain the face. For the ground bunk, pick someone who's on the low ration. They won't fight for long. Then trade that for the middle bunk. This time pick a leech. He'll have greased his way up there. Drag him down.

". . . By what right?"

I supposed that if he ever stopped to think about it, Lev would have found me much reduced, humanly. And this is what he suddenly seemed to be doing. To me, by now, violence was a neutral instrument. It wasn't even diplomacy by other means. It was currency, like tobacco, like bread. I told him,

By what right? The right to life. They call you a fascist. Now act like one.

Lev wouldn't do it. He stayed on the floor. And as a result he was always ill. "Pellagra," said Janusz, the young prisoner-doctor, and spread his hands. This was a deficiency that announced itself in the form of dermatitis, diarrhea, and disorganization of thought. With hot flushes in the frost of the tundra, with cold sweats in the cauldron of the barracks, and shivering, always shivering, Lev did hard labor in a strong brigade.

To one of Conrad's terse characterizations of Russian

life—"the frequency of the exceptional"—I would like to add another: the frequency of the total. Total states, with your sufferings selected, as if off a menu, by your sworn enemy.

I said, earlier, that I was in shock about Zoya—and that's true. It lasted until the day the sun came up. You could just see the corona, a pearly liquid smeared on the tundra's edge. The long eclipse was over: fingers pointed, and there was a grumbling, burbly cheer from the men. And I too came up out of eclipse and obscuration. I was no longer muffled in the chemicals of calm.

Now I started to look at my losses. And they were serious. I realized that there was nothing, now, nothing at all, that I liked to think about . . . Many more or less regrettable peccadilloes, in camp, were widely practiced; but onanism wasn't one of them. The urkas did it, and in public. And I suppose the younger rustics managed it for a while. For the rest of us it became a part of the past. Yet we all had the thoughts. I think we all still had the thoughts.

I still had them. Every night I staged my experiment. I would enter a room where Zoya lay sleeping. It was late afternoon. She was on the bed among star-bright pillows, in a petticoat or a short nightdress (here, and here only, some variation was allowed). I sat beside her and took her hand in mine. I kissed her lips. Then came the moment of transformation, when she rose up, flowed up, into my arms, and it began.

This nightly Fata Morgana used to feel like a source of strength—a reconnection with vital powers. But now it was weakening me, and corroding me. And as the sun worked its way up over the horizon I started saying it to myself, at first in a whisper of insomnia, then out loud in daylight, I started saying it: They didn't mean to do this, but that's what they've done. They've attacked my will. And that's all I've got.

You're a lucky boy, I told him.

It was his second rest day, and Lev sat scratching himself on the low wall in the yard. He squinted up at me and said, "Lucky how?"

I got my annual letter today. Kitty.

". . . Where is it?"

When I held it up Lev got to his feet—but he flinched and stepped back. I understood. At the moment of arrest you already feel halfway vanished. In prison you're a former person and already dead. In camp you're almost sure you've never been. Letters from home are like communications from an enfeebled medium, some ailing Madame Sosostris, with her tea leaves and her cracked Ouija board.

I can't show you the whole thing, I said. *I'm* the censor. But it's good news.

In Aesopian language Kitty told of Lev's arrest, and his expected departure for "an unknown destination." As a result of this second disappearance, the family had "unfortunately" lost the apartment. And Mother had lost her job.

Kitty went on to say that "the flu" was very virulent in the capital, and that Zoya and her mother had gone back to Kazan.

I said, Where the flu's less bad. And it's good news anyway.

He leaned into me and pressed his face to my chest.

"You make me very happy, brother. That's it—*get her out of town*. And I don't care what else Kitty said."

This was just as well. Kitty said that she thought it inconceivable that Zoya would "wait" for Lev. According to her, Zoya already had a new favorite at the Tech, and was "all over him" in the canteen. It is my solemn duty, Venus, to admit to the coarse joy this sentence gave me.

I said, What do you expect? It's Kitty.

"That's right. It's Kitty."

Yes, it was Kitty: that unreliable narrator. I wanted someone with greater authority to tell me it was true—about Zoya being all over her new favorite. I wanted someone like Georgi Zhukov or, better still, Winston Churchill to tell me it was true.

"Can you write back?" he said.

I'm supposed to be able to. But they don't like me. Anyway there's never anything to write with. Or write on.

"Why don't they like you? I mean, I can think of a reason or two. But why?"

The dogs.

"Ah. The dogs."

I was quite famous, in camp, for the way I dealt with the dogs. Most prisoners, including Lev, were horribly afraid of them. Not me. When I was a toddler we had a mule-sized borzoi. I can't even remember her; but she passed something on to me before she went. I have no fear of dogs. So I used to make them cringe. It's just a dog, imbued with a pig nature. It's just a snarl, waiting to become a cringe. I would often risk a beating to make the dogs cringe.

Lev said, "I went to the guardhouse and asked the pig. It says on my file: Without the Right to Correspondence. I thought that that was code for immediate execution. So did the pig. He kept peering at it and then peering at me. I don't have the right. But I'll keep on. I'll get it."

I said, untruthfully, I'm glad you don't worry about Kitty. And about Zoya.

"Worry? I'm good at worrying. When I started being her friend, before, I used to worry that someone was going to get her pregnant. But she didn't get pregnant. She can't. She had an abortion when she was sixteen and she can't. Then I worried that she was going to get arrested or kicked to death in the street. But other men, you mean? No. The thing about her . . . She's a hundred-percenter. And so am I, now. My uh, my status as a noncombatant. That's for her. That's for us."

You talk in riddles, Lev. Don't you understand that what you do here doesn't count?

"Doesn't it? Won't it? You don't see it, do you. It'll count."

On top of everything else there was also the huge brute, Arbachuk, who took a liking to my brother in what seemed to be the worst possible way. Every night he'd search him out. Why? To tousle him and taunt him and kiss him and tickle him. It was fashionable, at that time, for a brute to take a fascist as a pet, though Lev claimed it felt more like the other way around. "Suddenly I'm best friends with a mandrill," he said, which was game of him, because he was badly and rightly frightened. As Arbachuk shouldered his way through the barracks, with his tattoos and his moist, gold-flecked smile, Lev would close his eyes for a second and the light would pass from his face. All I could do about Arbachuk was indicate, with a glance and a movement of the shoulders, that if it really came to it he would have to get by me too. Lev said that it was much worse when I wasn't there. So I always was. And when I couldn't be, we relied on Semyon or Johnreed, two of the higher-ranking officer veterans, a colonel and a captain, who were both Heroes of the Soviet Union—an honor of which, on arrest, they were naturally stripped . . . You're probably wondering about that name: Johnreed. A lot of people his age were called Johnreed, after John Reed, the author of *Ten Days That Shook the World*. There were so many Johnreeds in camp that they had earned the status of a phylum, the *Johnreeds*, like the *Americans* and, later, the *Doctors*—the Jewish doctors. In its stirred account of the October Revolution, John Reed's book barely mentioned Joseph Vissarionovich, so he banned it, thus whipping out the carpet, so to speak, from under all the Johnreeds.

Arbachuk used to bring titbits for Lev, who always

refused them. Not just chunks of bread, either, but meat—mince, sausage—and on one occasion an *apple*. "I'm not hungry," Lev would say. I couldn't believe it: he sat there with Arbachuk's tongue in his ear, and half a pork chop dangling under his nose, saying, "I'm not hungry."

"Open!" said Arbachuk, squeezing the bolts of Lev's jaw in his hand.

"I'm not hungry. This tattoo, Citizen. I can only see the last word. What does it say?"

Slowly and grimly Arbachuk rolled up his sleeve. And there were the bruised letters: *You may live but you won't love.*

"One bite. Open!"

"I eat the full ration. I'm not hungry, Citizen. I work in a strong brigade."

Like the kind of man who cannot forget or forgive a woman's past, and must sit her down, every other night, and have her go through the hoops all over again ("He touched you *where*? You kissed his *what*?"), I would come to Lev, seeking the narrative of greatest pain. I know about that kind of man, because I'm him—he's me. In later years it was the only way I could tell for sure that I was finding a woman interesting: I would want her to confess, to denounce, to inform. And they quite enjoyed it at first, because it felt like attention. They soon came to dread it. They soon caught on . . . This trait of mine didn't really have the time or the opportunity to get started between war and camp. You see, nearly all the ex-lovers of nearly all my girlfriends—they were dead. And I didn't mind the dead. It would be a strange kind of Russian who didn't forgive the dead. I didn't mind the dead. The living were what bothered me.

When, shortly before I was arrested, Lev asked for my permission to try his luck with Zoya, I didn't even take the trouble to laugh in his face. I gave him the trisyllabic *You?;* and that was all. I honestly didn't give it a moment's thought. But Lev was like clever little brothers everywhere. He watched what I did and then tried the opposite. He came at Zoya without intensity.

Oh well *done*, I said, during one of our last conversations in freedom. You're her errand boy. And her mascot.

"That's it," he said, stuttering. He was always stuttering. "Come on, how close did *you* ever get to her? Me, I'm there in the room. I'm there all the time. I'm there when she's *changing*."

Changing?

"Behind the curtain."

How big is the curtain? And how thick?

"Thick. It goes from the floor up to here. She drapes clothes over the top of it."

What clothes?

"Petticoats and things."

Jesus Christ . . . And now she's fucking that linguist. I don't know how you can bear it.

"Oh, I can bear it."

This went on for nearly a year—a year in which Zoya had

three more affairs. "One a term," he now told me. And it was while he was sitting there, in the conical attic, holding her hand, and talking her through her latest misadventure, that Lev made his next move.

"I said it teasingly. I said, 'You're unlucky in love because you're drawn to the wrong men. These head-in-air types. Try a slightly smaller, uglier one. Like me. We're so much keener.' She laughed, and then went silent for five seconds. Then next time I said it, she laughed and went silent for ten seconds. And so on. And then she had another."

Another what?

"Another affair. A whole other one."

Is it possible, I said, that you and I have a drop of blood in common? Weren't you jealous?

"Jealous? I couldn't have borne it for a minute if I'd been *jealous*. I didn't have the right to be jealous. In whose name? I was too busy learning."

I waited.

"Learning what I'd have to do to keep her."

. . . You dirty little *bastard*.

It does happen. In my life I've seen perhaps three examples of it. And you, Venus, are one of them. You and that Roger. As I said at the time, possibly rather unfeelingly, *You're about three-quarters trained to think that everyone looks the same. That's the illusion your crowd is foisting on itself. So you think it's snobbish not to fancy cripples. And now you've got that sick bat trailing after you*. I still think that that's what it mainly was, Venus: pity and piety. You told me there were compensations, and I believed you. You spoke of his gratitude—his gratitude, and your relief from certain cares. And I can see that obviously attractive women sometimes do get to the end of obviously attractive men: their entitlements, their expectations, their unexceptionable hearts. And so one morning the princess kisses the bullfrog, and finds it good.

Then what?

"It was a Sunday. Late afternoon. We were lying there and I said it again. Then she went all still. Then she stood up and took—"

Enough. Took her clothes off, I suppose.

"She already had her clothes off. Most of them. No, she took my—"

Enough.

They had nine months; and then, as Lev's classmates and professors were being hauled in one after the other, it was she who took the decision. They activated the scrofulous rabbi in his basement. It was clandestine, and I suppose of doubtful legitimacy. But they stamped on the glass, wrapped in its handkerchief—the destruction of the temple, the renunciation of earlier ties. And they made the vows.

One scrap of comfort was given to me (and there are these leftovers of comfort, at the banquet of sorrow). Its efficacy will perhaps be obscure to those accustomed to the exercise of free will. I learned that Zoya, while not indifferent to older men (she came close to scandal with a newly married thirty-year-old), never involved herself with any of my closest peers: veterans. So I could tell myself that when we kissed, and she retained my lower lip for a second between her big square teeth, the taste she didn't like was the ferrous hormone of war.

It comforted me because I could attribute my failure to historical forces, along with everything else. History did it.

Reveille, in camp, was achieved as follows: a metal bludgeon, wielded by a footlike hand, would clatter up and down for a full minute between two parallel iron rails. This you never got used to. Each morning, as you girded yourself in the yard, you would stare at the simple contraption and wonder at its acoustical might. I now know that, for some barbarous reason (the quicker detection, perhaps, of even the tiniest animal), hunger sharpens the hearing. But it didn't just get louder—it grew in shrillness and, somehow, in articulacy. The sound seemed to trumpet the dawn of a new dominion (more savage, more stupid, more certain) and to repudiate the laxity and amateurism of the day before.

Until Lev came to camp my first thought, on waking, was always the same thought, admitting of no modulation. It was always: I would give my eyesight for just ten more seconds . . . Another day has been cranked up in front of you; the day itself, the dark dawn (the glassy sheen of the sector and the chalklike mist which the lungs refused), looked like the work of a team of laborers, a nightshift—the result of hours of toil. The cold is waiting for me, I'd think; it is expecting me, and everything is prepared. Don't you find, my dear, when you step out into the rain, that you always have a moment's grace before feeling the first few dots on your hair? Cold isn't like that. Cold is cold, obviously, and wants all your heat. It is on you. It grips and frisks you for all your heat.

Then, after Lev came, daily consciousness would arrive to find me yanked upright on my boards. The pig would still be belaboring the iron rails as I dropped to the floor. I was always the first man out of the hut—and always with the feeling that a lurid but sizable treat lay ahead of me. What was this treat, exactly? It was to get my first glimpse of Lev, and to see the way his frown softened into the flesh of his brow. It wouldn't happen the moment he set eyes on me. He would smile his strained—his stretched—smile, but the frown, the inverted chevron of care, would remain awhile and then fade, like a gauge measuring my power to reassure. And sometimes I feel that I was never closer to the crest than during those exchanges or transfusions—never more alive.

Now that sounds all right, doesn't it? Lurid, then, in what way? I see that I cannot avoid the lurid. Another sun had risen in me. This sun was black, and its rays, its spokes, were made of hope and hate.

Lev, by the way, didn't last long in his brigade—the strong brigade under Markargan. Even though he was by now very fit. Very sick and very fit: you could be that there, and go on being it for quite a while. But no. It was a rare fascist who lasted long in a strong brigade. In a strong brigade there was a unanimity of effort that had the weight of a union contract or a military oath: you met the norm and you ate the full ration. It was one way of getting through it—the booming worksong, the bucketful of soup, the sleep of the dead. A peasant, carrying around with him his millennium of slave ethic—a peasant could manage it without great inner cost. But an *intelligent* . . . This is what comes over you, in the slave system. It takes a couple of months. It builds, like a graduated panic attack. It is this: the absorption of the fact that despite your obvious innocence of any crime, the exaction of the penalty is not inadvertent. Now go with such a thought to a strong brigade. You try and you try, but the idea that you are *excelling* in the service of the state—it weighs your hands down, and causes them to drop to your side. You can feel your hands as they drop to your side; your sides, your hips, feel them as they fall. Needless to say, a weak brigade, with its shiteater short commons, wasn't any good either. So what do you do? You do what all the fascists do. You skive and slack and fake and wheedle, and you subsist.

Once he was off the full ration, Lev's bowel infection got worse. In camp, even hospitalization for dysentery obeyed the law of the norm; and by early 1949 Lev could meet it. And what was the norm? The norm was more blood than shit. More blood than shit. He went to Janusz, who gave him some pills and promised him a bed. On the day before his admission, Lev had some sort of shouting match in his barracks, over a sewing needle (that is, a fishbone), and was immediately denounced—his name dropped into the suggestion box outside the guardhouse. Instead of a week in the infirmary he had a week in the isolator, wearing underclothes, and crouched on a bench above knee-deep bilge.

The frequency of the total. The total state—the masterpiece of misery.

That week had a turbulent color for me. You will recall my "proof," framed in the autumn of 2001, on the nonexistence of God, and how pleased I was with it. "Never mind, for now, about famine, flood, pestilence, and war: if God really cared about us, he would never have given us religion." But this loose syllogism is easily exploded, and all questions of theodicy simply disappear—if God is a Russian.

And we the people keep coming back for more. We fucking love it. That week had an awful color for me, but when Lev came out, walking the way he did, and with his head at that angle, I more or less accepted the fact that Norlag wouldn't kill him, not on its own. He could bear it.

3.

"The Fascists Are Beating Us!"

"What worries me about me," he said (this was half a year later), "is what kind of shape I'll be in when and if I get out. I don't just mean how thin or how ill. Or how *old*. I mean up here. In the head. You know what I think I'm turning into?"

A moron.

"Exactly. Good. So it's not just me."

We all have it.

"Then that's bad. Because it probably means it's true. My thoughts—they're not really thoughts anymore. They're impulses. It's all on the level of cold, hot. Cold soup, hot soup. What will I talk to my wife about? All I'll be thinking is cold soup, hot soup."

You'll be talking to her like you're talking to me.

"But it's so *tiring* talking to you. You know what I mean. Christ. Imagine if we weren't here. I mean together."

The evening was warm and bright, and we sat smoking on the steps of the toy factory. Yes, the toy factory, because the economy of the camp was as various as the economy of the state. We churned out everything from uranium to teaspoons. I myself was mass-producing threadbare clockwork rabbits with sticks in their paws and little snare drums attached to their waists.

Two youngish prisoners strolled past at a donnish pace, one with his hands clasped behind his back, the other ponderously gesturing.

"All I care about, in the end," the second man was saying, "is tits."

"No," said the other. "No, not tits. Arses."

". . . New boys," said Lev.

I shrugged. Young men, after their arrival, would talk about sex and even sports for a couple of weeks, then about sex and food, then about food and sex, then about food.

Lev yawned. His color was better now. He had had his time in the infirmary, and a course of weak penicillin from Janusz. But his lips and nails were blue, from hunger, not cold, and he had the brownish pigmentation around the mouth, deeper than any suntan. We all had that too, the great-ape muzzle.

"It's hard to do when you're covered in lice," he said, "but it's good to think about sex."

I'm very sorry to say, Venus, that this was by now, for me, an *extremely* sensitive subject. You see, I had managed to persuade myself that Lev's bond with Zoya was largely a thing of the spirit. It was, in fact, pretty well platonic. What a relief for her, I told myself, after all those passionate ups and downs. And I could even derive some pleasure from imagining the kind of evening that must surely be their norm. The remains of the simple supper cleared away, the taking of turns at the washbasin, Gretel, a little shyly, slipping into her bedsocks and coarse nightgown, Hansel sighing in his vest and longjohns, the peck on the cheek, and then over they turned, back to back, each with a complacent grunt, and sought their rightful rest . . . And while Lev lay in his little death, the other Zoya, the sweating succubus, rose up like a mist and came to me.

"But it's not really *thought*, is it. It's more like cold soup, hot soup."

There *is* poetry, I said.

"True. There is poetry. I can sometimes work on a line or two for half a minute. Then there's a jolt and I'm back to the other stuff."

I told him about the thirty-year-old professor in the women's block. She recited *Eugene Onegin* to herself every day.

"Every day? Yeah, but some days you don't *want* to read the . . . the fucking *Bronze Horseman*."

That's right. Some days you don't *want* to read the . . . the fucking *Song of Igor's Campaign*.

"That's right. Some days you don't *want* to read the . . ."

And so we got through another hour, before we groped our way to our bedding.

Then came the changes. But before I get to that, it is necessary for me to describe a brief internal detour: a lucky break. I suggest, my dear, that you take full advantage of this interlude or breather, using it, perhaps, to tabulate my better qualities. Because I am soon going to be doing some very bad things.

We never saw the Chief Administrator, Kovchenko, but we heard about him—his polar-bear fur coat, his groin-high sealskin boots, his fishing trips and reindeer hunts, his parties. Every so often a card would appear on the bulletin board, asking for the services of inmate musicians, actors, dancers, athletes, whom he used to entertain his guests (fellow chief administrators or inspectorates from the center). After their performance, the artistes were given a vat of leftovers. Excitingly, many came back sick from overeating, and there were a number of fatal gorgings.

One day Kovchenko posted a signed request for "any inmate with experience of installing a 'television.'" I had never installed a television; but I had dissected one, at the Tech. I told Lev what I remembered about it, and we applied. Nothing happened for a week. Then they called out our names, and fed us and scrubbed us, and jeeped us out to Kovchenko's estate.

Lev and I stood waiting, under guard, in what I would now call a gazebo, a heated octagonal outhouse, with a workbench and an array of tools. Kovchenko entered, gaunt and oddly professorial in his jodhpurs and tweed jacket. A metal crate was solemnly wheeled in, and two men who looked like gardeners began unbolting it. "Gentlemen," said Kovchenko, breathing deeply and noisily, "prepare to see the future." Up came the lid and in we peered: a formless, gray-black sludge of valves and tubes and wires.

So we started going there every day. Every day we came out of the thick breath of the camp and entered a world of room temperature, picture windows, ample food, coffee, American cigarettes, and continuous fascination.

After two months we put together something that looked like an especially disgraceful deep-sea fish, plus, on the open back porch, a pylon of aerials. All we ever raised, on the screen, were fleeting representations of the ambient weather: night blizzards, slanting sleet against a charcoal void. Once, in the presence of the chief, we picked up what might or might not have been a test card. This satisfied Kovchenko, whose expectations were no longer high. The set was transported to the main house. We later heard that it was put on a plinth in the entrance hall, for display, like a piece of ancient metalwork or a brutalist sculpture.

We too had wanted to see the future. Now we returned to the past—to the ball-bearings works, in fact, where you just went *oompah* every five seconds, and thought about cold soup, hot soup. I became convinced, around then, that boredom was the second pillar of the system—the first being terror. At school, Venus, we were taught by people who were prepared to lie to children for a living; you sat there listening to information you knew to be false (even my mother's school was no different). Later on you discovered that all the interesting subjects were so hopelessly controversial that no one dared study them. Public discourse was boring, the papers and the radio were just a drone in the other room, and the meetings were boring, and all talk outside the family was boring, because no one could say what came naturally. Bureaucracy was boring. Queuing was boring. The most stimulating place in Russia was the Butyrki prison in Moscow. I can see why they needed the terror, but why did they need the boredom?

That was the big zona. This was the little zona, the slave-labor end of it. In freedom, every non-nomenklatura citizen knew perpetual hunger—the involuntary slurp and gulp of the esophagus. In camp, your hunger kicked as I imagine a fetus would kick. It was the same with boredom. And *boredom*, by now, has lost all its associations with mere lassitude and vapidity. Boredom is no longer the absence of emotion; it is itself an emotion, and a violent one. A silent tantrum of boredom.

Another thing that happened, on the credit side, is that we both grew close to Janusz, the prisoner-doctor. He did everything he could for us—and just to stand next to him for ten minutes made you feel marginally less unhealthy. Tall, broad, and twenty-four years old, he had a head of jungly black hair that grew with anarchic force; we used to say that any barber, going in there, would want danger money. Janusz was a Jewish doctor who was trapped in an imposture. He wasn't pretending that he was a Christian (no great matter either way, in camp). He was pretending that he was a doctor. And he wasn't—not yet. Always the most difficult position. And it wouldn't have been so hard for him if he hadn't been kind, very kind, continuously moved by all he saw. For those early operations he had to feel his way into it, into the human body, with his knife. First, do no harm.

Trucks and troops went the word. Trucks and troops. That meant Moscow, and policy change. A decision had been arrived at in the Central Committee, and it came down to us in the form of headlights and machineguns.

At all times and in all seasons the camp population was in flux, with various multitudes being reshuffled, released, reimprisoned, shipped out, shipped in (and it was amazing, by the way, that my brother and I were separated just once, and then for barely a year). Our business, now, was to gaze into this motion arithmetic, and try to discern something that could be called an *intention* . . .

Lev was standing by the barracks window, looking out, and bobbing minutely up and down—his way of discharging unease. He said,

"Listen. Arbachuk cornered me behind the woodshop last night. I thought I was finally going to get raped, but no. He was speechless, he was all stricken and mournful. Then he reached down and squeezed my hand . . . He's been like that before. But now I think he was saying goodbye. They're shipping out the brutes."

I said that that had to be good for us.

"Why good?" He turned. "Since when do they make it good for us? I know how to stay alive here. As it is. What's next?"

We were confined to barracks and spent our days looking out, looking out. And you didn't want to be in the zona, not now, with its dogs and columns of men and the new disposition of forces. The watchtowers—their averted searchlights and their domes like army helmets with a spray of gun barrels set under the peak, at right angles, like scurvied teeth . . . At such times, I often thought I was playing in a sports match, ice hockey, say, in slow motion (dreamlike yet lethal, zero-sum, sudden-death); and that I was the goalkeeper—excluded from the action except when responding to hideous emergencies.

They isolated the brutes, and trucked them out—the simplest way, we supposed, of ending the war between the brutes and the bitches. But then they isolated the bitches, too. And as soon as the bitches were gone, they isolated the locusts, and then the leeches. If you discounted the shit-eaters, who remained, that left the politicals and the informers—the fascists and the snakes.

Lev said, looking out, "Christ, how clear does it need to be? They're isolating *us*."

. . . We're all going to be freed, I said.

"It's just as likely," said Lev, "that we're all going to be shot."

Over the next few weeks our sector, freshly depopulated, started filling up again. And all the new arrivals were fascists. They were isolating *us*. Why? Why were they giving us, systemwide, exactly what we wanted—delivering us, awakening us?

To read the mind of Moscow, in 1950, this was where you would have needed to be: in the antennae, in the control turret, of the slug that was unmethodically devouring the leader's brain. We weren't in that turret. I say this with a shrug, but the best guess, now, is that Joseph Vissarionovich had started to fear for the ideological integrity of the common felon.

The power ascribed to us, even the power of contamination, wasn't real (we were not yet a force). Now the power was telling us it was there. The process took about a month. We were like blind men recovering their sight. It was a question of eyes turning to other eyes, and holding them. Self-awareness dawned. The politicals looked from face to face—and became political.

Two things followed from this. The policy change in Moscow meant the end, the unintended suicide, of the slave-labor system. It also meant that Lev and I became enemies. A decision is made, around a table, in a room a thousand miles away—and a pair of brothers must go to war. This, Venus, is the meaning, the hour-by-hour import, of political systems.

But I'm not going to waste your time with the politics. I'll give you what you need to know. And I'm afraid I cannot neglect to tell the tale of the guard called Uglik—the strenuous tale of Comrade Uglik. Looking back, I now see what the politics was: the politics of Siamese twins, and mermen, and bearded ladies. It was the politics of the slug called arteriosclerosis.

"The fascists are beating us! The fascists are beating us!"

This cry (not without a certain charm, even then) was often to be heard during the summer of 1950. We started beating the snakes, the one-in-tens. No longer would they tarry at their tables in the mess hall, kissing bunched fingertips over their double rations. Now, when they made their way across the square to the guardhouse, it was not to top up their denunciations for an extra cigarette: it was to plead for sanctuary in the punishment block—with its shin-deep bilge, its obese bedbugs.

Our favored method of chastisement was called "tossing." It was what the peasants used to do, mindful, as ever, of scarce materials. Don't blunt that knife, don't strain that cudgel: let gravity do it. One man per limb, three preparatory swings, up they went, like a caber, and down they crashed. Then we tossed them again. Until they no longer flailed in the air. We left them out there for the pigs: canvas bagfuls of broken bones.

You seem displeased, brother, I said, as I strode into the barracks dusting my palms.

"You're not my brother."

I waited. Everyone flocked and scrambled to witness a tossing. Not Lev, who always withdrew.

"What I'm saying," he said, "is that you're unrecognizable. You're like Vad. Do you know that? You've joined the herd. Suddenly you're just like everybody else."

This was perfectly true. I was unrecognizable. In a matter of weeks I had become a Stakhanovite of agitation, a "shock" stirrer and mixer—demands and demonstrations, pickets, petitions, protests, provocations. Ah, you're thinking: displacement, transference; the mechanism of sublimation. And it is true that I was deliberately embracing the chemical heat of mass emotion, and the infuriant of power. But I never lost sight of a possible outcome, and a possible future.

"I ask you to consider my position. You've chosen a path, you and your herd," he was saying. "Violence and escalation. You know fucking well what's going to happen."

For a very brief period it looked as though the isolation of the politicals, as a policy, had a subtext: we were to be worked to death (less food, longer hours). But the pigs still had their quotas, and now they had given us the weapon of the strike.

Anyway, I was in a position to say, with some indignation, Oh, I get it. You want the sixteen-hour day and the punitive ration. Well we don't.

"You won that fight. Christ, that was eight or nine fights ago. And the pigs, they aren't going to keep on backing off. You know what's going to happen. Or maybe you don't. Because you're running with the herd. Look at you. Thundering along with it."

Again I waited.

"What you're going to get is a war with the state. A fight

to the death against Russia. Against the Cheka and the Red Army. And you're going to win that, are you?"

I didn't say so, but I always knew what was coming our way. I always knew.

"All right. I'll ask you for the last time. And I'm asking a lot. There are three or four men here who have a chance of bringing the herd to a halt. And you're one of them. Please consider my position. I have to ask. And it's the last time that I'll ask you anything as a brother."

You ask the moon, Lev.

"Then some of us will die," he said, turning his eyes away from mine and folding his arms.

We haven't all of us got a good reason to live, I said. Some of us will die. And some of us won't.

I know how you feel about violence. I knew how you felt about it right from the start. The film on TV, in the Chicago den, was in fact a comedy; but a punch was thrown, and a nose dripped blood. You ran in tears from the room. And as you swung the door inward the brass knob caught you full in the eye. That's how tall you were when you found out the world was hard.

On New Year's Day, 1951, the authorities retaliated: three men from our center were confined to the main punishment block, where thirty or forty informers had found refuge. The informers, we heard, would that night be issued with axes and alcohol, and the cells would all be unlocked.

So we at once sent a message. We too changed our policy. We stopped beating the snakes. We stopped beating them, and started killing them. I did three.

Now, pluck out your Western eyes. Pluck them out, and reach for the other pair . . . These others are not the eyes of a Temachin or a Hulagu, hooded and aslant, nor those of Ivan the Terrible, paranoid and pious, nor those of Vladimir Ilich, both childish and horizon-seeking.* No, these others are the eyes of the old city-peasant (drastically urbanized), on her hands and knees at the side of the road, witness to starvation and despair, to permanent and universal injustice, to innumerable enormities. Eyes that say: enough . . . But now I see your eyes before me, as they really are (the long brown irises, the shamingly clean whites); and they threaten the decisive withdrawal of love, just as Lev's did, half a century ago. All right. In setting my story down I create a mirror. I see me, myself. Look at his face. Look at his *hands*.

Lev once saw me fresh from a killing: my second. He described the encounter to me, years later. I give his memory of it, his version—because I haven't got a memory. I haven't got a version.

Badged with blood, and panting like a dog that has run all

* Temachin is Genghis Khan; the Mongol warlord Hulagu is his grandson. Vladimir Ilich is Lenin, leader of Russia, 1917–24.

day, I pushed past Lev at the entrance to the latrine; I slapped my raised forearm against the wall and dropped my head on it, and with the other hand I clawed at the string around my waist, then emptied my bladder with gross copiousness and (I was told) a snarl of gratitude. I paused and made another sound: an open-mouthed exhalation as I whipped my head to the right, freeing my brow from the tickling heat of my forelock. I looked up. I remember this. He was staring at me with bared teeth and a frown that went half an inch deep. He pointed, directing my attention to the frayed belt, the lowered trousers. I find I can't avoid asking you to imagine what he saw.

"I know where you've been," he said. "You've been at the wet stuff."

Which is what we called it: killing. The wet stuff.

I said, Well someone's got to do it. Hut Three, Prisoner 47. His conscience was unclean.

"His conscience was *not* unclean. That's the point."

What are you *talking* about?

"Look at your eyes. You're like an Old Believer. Ah, kiss the cross, brother. Kiss the cross."

Kissing the cross: this was fraternal shorthand for religious observance. Because that's what they did, in church, before Christianity was illegalized (along with all the others): they kissed it, the death instrument. Lev was telling me that my mind was no longer free. It was all of a piece that my sense of it, then, wasn't mental but physical. I was a slave who had got his body back. And now I was offering it up again—freely. That's all true. But I was never without the other thought and the other calculation.

Years later, in a very different phase of my existence, sitting on a hotel balcony, in Budapest, and drinking beer and eating nuts and olives after a shower, and before going out for a late-night meeting with a ladyfriend, I read the famous memoir by the poet Robert von Ranke Graves (English father, German mother). I was very struck, and very comforted, by his admission that it took him ten years to recover, morally, from the First World War. But it took me rather longer than that to recover from the Second. He spent his convalescent decade on some island in the Mediterranean. I spent mine above the Arctic Circle, in penal servitude.

It was a while before I worked out what he meant, Lev, when he said of the murdered snake that "his conscience was *not* unclean. That's the point." . . . In freedom, in the big zona, the informer ruined lives. In camp, in the little zona, the informer worsened, and sometimes shortened, lives that were already ruined. Anonymous denunciation, for self-betterment: you can tell it's profoundly criminal, and profoundly Russian, because only Russian criminals think it isn't. All other criminals, the world over, think it is. But Russian criminals—from Dostoevsky's fellow inmates ("an informer is not subjected to the slightest humiliation; the thought never occurs to anyone to react indignantly towards him") to the current president, yes, to Vladimir Vladimirovich (who has expressed simple dismay at the idea of doing without his taiga of poison pens)—think it isn't.* For my part, then, in the extermination of the snakes, I am guilty on the following count: they knew what they were doing, but they didn't know that what they were doing was wrong. "The fascists are beating us! The fascists are beating us!" Now I see the obscure charm—the pathos of that scandalized cry. And then we stopped beating them, and started killing them. I did three. I couldn't have done a fourth. Nevertheless, I did three.

The camp was more war, Venus, more war, and the moral rot of war . . . The war between the brutes and the bitches was a civil or sectarian war. The war between the snakes and the fascists was a proxy war. Now that the snakes were gone (siphoned off as a class), the battle lines were forming for a revolutionary war: the war between the fascists and the pigs.

Lev was an innocent bystander in the first war (as we all were), and he was a conscientious objector in the second war. No one could avoid the third war. And early on he took a wound.

* Dostoevsky was imprisoned from 1849 to 1853, for sedition. Vladimir Vladimirovich is Putin, leader of Russia since 1999.

4.

"Meet Comrade Uglik"

The pigs.

They were all semiliterate, but even I could remember the tail end of a time when the pigs were as humanly various as the prisoners—cruel, kind, indifferent. We had other things in common. They were almost as frozen, starving, filthy, disease-ridden, slave-driven, and terrorized as we were. But by now they had evolved. They were second-generation: pigs, and the sons of pigs. And what you saw was the emergence of human beings of a new type. Such was Comrade Uglik.

I shadowed my brother, over the years, and did some quiet roughing-up on his behalf. But there wasn't anything I could have done about Uglik. He was just Lev's bad luck.

I asked him, Why are you crying?

These were the first words I had addressed to Lev in ten or eleven months. By this time (January 1953), his level in camp was on a par with the shiteaters—or lower still, for a while, because the shiteaters were merely pitied and then ignored, and Lev was ostracized. There were people who had a bit more respect for him now. Something to do with his size and shape—the little bent figure, the sloping shoulders under the crumpled face, and always alone, aloof, against. Chinless, of course, but the whole set of him as defiant as a barrel-jawed dwarf in a city street. He wouldn't cross a picket line or walk away from a sit-down or anything like that. The offense he was giving was moral and passive and silent. He wouldn't partake of the ambient esprit. He just wouldn't come to the well. Lev, now, was twenty-four.

I asked him, Why are you crying?

He flinched, as if my voice, grown unfamiliar, held a hardness for him. Or else, perhaps, he had some sense of the unholy brew of motives that lay behind my question . . . Of all the freedoms we had secured over the past eighteen months, the one that mattered most to me, I found, was the removal of the number from my back. The one that mattered to Lev was his right to correspondence. *His* right: not anybody else's. He campaigned for it alone, and he won it alone; and for this too he was shunned. Now he was sitting on a tree stump in the copse behind the infirmary, Zoya's first letter in one hand and his dripping face in the other. If you'd asked me whether I hoped that everything was over between them, the truth-drug answer would have been something like, Well, that would be a *start*. But I hope she hasn't done it nicely. That might not do me any good at all.

"I'm crying . . ." He bowed his head, becoming absorbed by the task of returning the sheath of tissuey paper to its wrinkled pouch; but every time he neared success he had to raise a finger to wipe the itch off his nose. "I'm crying," he said, "because I'm so *dirty*."

I paused. I said, And all else is well?

"Yes. No. There is talk, in freedom, of Birobidzhan. They're building barracks in Birobidzhan."

Birobidzhan was a region on the northeastern border of China—largely, and wisely, uninhabited. Ever since the 1930s there had been talk of resettling the Jews in Birobidzhan.

"They're building barracks for them in Birobidzhan. Janusz thinks they're going to hang the Jewish doctors in Red Square. The country is hysterical with it, the press . . . And then the Jews will run the gauntlet to Birobidzhan. Now if you'll excuse me. This will take about a minute."

And for about a minute he wept, he musically wept. He was crying, he said, because he was so dirty. I believed him. Being so dirty made you cry more often than being so cold or being so hungry. We weren't so cold or so hungry, not anymore. But we were so dirty. Our clothes were stiff, practically wooden, barklike, with dirt. And under the wood, woodlice and woodworm.

"Ah, that's better. It beats me how the women stay so clean," he went on, as if talking to himself. "Maybe they lick themselves, like cats. And we're like dogs that just roll in the shit. Now," he said and turned to me. "I have a dilemma. Perhaps you can help me resolve it."

He focused and smiled—the pretty teeth. I found I still feared that smile.

"Here," he said, "is no good. I can't stay here. I'm leaving. I'm off. It's no good *here*. Here, everybody's going to die."

I said, There comes a time when you have to—

"Oh don't give me that. Every man in the camp can give me that. The thing is that I'm urgently needed in freedom. To protect my wife. So. Two choices. I can escape."

Where to? Birobidzhan?

"I can escape. Or I can inform."

I said, Today we go to the bathhouse.

"Come on, take me seriously. Think it through, think it through. If I inform, it's conceivable I'll be pardoned. With things as they are now. You know, give them a list of all the strike leaders. I could try that. Then you could kill me. And do you know what you'd get if you killed me?" He closed his eyes and nodded and opened them again. "You'd get a hard-on."

I said, Today we go to the bathhouse.

He looked at the ground, saying, "And that's another reason to cry."

The two of us always went to the bathhouse together. Even when we weren't speaking or meeting each other's eyes. The thing had to be done in relay. Now you'd think that the bathhouse was where we all wanted to go, but many men would risk a beating to avoid it or even delay it. None of our innumerable agitations had any effect in the bathhouse. For instance, it was quite possible to come out even dirtier than you went in. One of the reasons for this was institutional or systemic: an absence of soap. There was not always an absence of water, but there was always, it seemed, an absence of soap. Even in 1991 the coalminers went on strike for soap. There was *never* any soap in the USSR.

We were queueing in the sleet. Then suddenly there were a hundred of us in a changing room with hooks for twelve. And suddenly there was soap—little black globules, doled out of a bucket. At this point everything but your overcoat got thrown into the pot, to be redistributed later on at random; but by taking turns we could guard our most precious things—the spare foot-rag, the extra spoon. Lev filed through first, with his mug of warm water. I gazed at my black globule. I held it to my nose. It smelt as if some sacred physical law had been demeaned in its creation.

It was then I noticed it, in the pocket of the leaden wad I held in my arms: Lev's letter . . . After four years of war and nearly seven years of camp, my integrity, some might feel, had come under a certain strain. A for-the-duration rapist (or so it then seemed), a coldblooded (but also tumescent) executioner, I intended, when I ever thought about it, to go back to being the kind of man I was in 1941. And now, of course, I weep to think that I imagined this was possible. The kind of man who drew a shopkeeper's attention to the fact that he had undercharged; the kind of man who gave up his seat for the elderly and infirm; the kind of man who would never read the last page of a novel first, but would get there by honest means; and so on. But there was Zoya's letter, and I reached for it.

There are self-interested and utilitarian reasons for

behaving well, it turns out. I had some bad times in camp, clearly enough, but those five minutes, under the brown mists of the bathhouse, bred half a century of pain . . . Family news (her mother's poor health, his mother's improvement), that new job in the textiles factory, Kazan, the idea of a "homeland" in the east, earnest and repetitive protestations of love: all that was over in the first paragraph. The remainder, four dense sides, was of course Aesopian in style, with the fable unfolding in three stages. She described the arrangement of a vase of flowers, and then the preparation and consumption of an enormous meal. It was easily translated: a marathon preen (with much posing and primping), a saturnalia of foreplay, and a contortionist's black mass of coition. Even her handwriting, tiny though it was, looked completely indecent, wanton—lost to shame.

Lev came out and I went in.

The conjugal visits, in the House of Meetings, had not yet begun. His was three and a half years away.

Lev's brigade, that morning (February 14, 1953), had been reassigned and reequipped, and was late starting out. The pigs stopped the column as it was crossing the sector. And one of them said,

"We have a distinguished visitor. Gentlemen? Meet Comrade Uglik."

Uglik? Take away the uniform (and the riding boots and

neckerchief), and he looked more like an urka than a pig. And the urkas, it had to be said, were physically vivid. You sometimes caught yourself thinking that if human life ended anyway at twenty-five, then an urka might seem a reasonable thing to be. Whereas, with the pigs, the only suggestion of moisture and mobility in their gray, closed faces was the vague lavatorial humidity that came off them when they were roused. Uglik was with us for only a week, and was active among us for only a day and a night. But no one ever forgot him.

His face was sleek, and rosily sensual, with rich, moist, outward-tending lips. His eyes were positively flamboyant. Looking at those eyes, you felt not just fear but also the kind of depression that would normally take a week to build. His eyes were wearyingly vigorous. Uglik, I think, came from the future. Hitherto, the standard janitor of the Gulag was a product of the sleeping residuum to be found in all societies: they were sadists and subnormals (and the palest and dankest onanists), now hugely empowered; and in their best moments, their moments of clarity and candor, they all knew it. That was why they would far rather torment a cosmologist or a ballet dancer than a rapist or a murderer. They wanted someone good. Raised as a pig, by a pig, Uglik was different. *He'd* never felt subnormal. And freedom from conscious shame had given him the leisure to develop as an extrovert. He was, on the other hand, an alcoholic. That was why he was here, as demotion and punishment for a string of disgraces at various camps in South Central Asia. They were sending us their lost men. At this point Uglik had two months to live.

"Meet Comrade Uglik." The guards stopped the work team—Lev's work team—and Comrade Uglik was asked to inspect it. He moved from scarecrow to scarecrow, gracefully, with a bend of the knees and a courtly smile—as if, said Lev, he was choosing a partner for a dance. Which he was. He wanted his partner to be young and strong, because he wanted the dance to last a long time. At last he settled on the candidate (Rovno, the big Ukrainian), and the infraction (improper headgear). Then Uglik flexed his upraised fingers into a pair of black leather gloves.

A pig would usually beat you more or less according to method, like a man chopping down a tree. Uglik of course intended to mount a display, and he did so, with many stylish feints and swivels, and with a toreador's tight-buttocked saunters—little intervals for tacit applause. He was not very fat and very mottled—indeed, at this hour, he was not yet breathing and sweating very heavily, he was not yet very drunk . . . It went wrong for Lev when someone near him shouted out—a single word, and, in the circumstances, the worst word possible. The word was *queer*. Uglik's head turned toward him, Lev said, like a weathercock whipped around by the wind. He came forward. He picked Lev, I think, because this time he wanted someone small. A double blow to the ears with the stiffened palms of the hand. Everyone there remembered an echoing slap, but Lev remembered a detonation.

This was not the last of Uglik's achievements during his short time among us. Late in the evening he visited the women's block. There he also applied himself: he didn't rape—he just beat. And finally, on his way back to the guardhouse, he succeeded in falling over and blacking out under the wooden portals of the toy factory. Uglik spent five hours in forty degrees of frost. He had his gloves on.

Rovno, the giant farmboy, soon recovered. As for Lev—that night in the barracks, flat on his back, he had two worms of bloody phlegm coiling out of his head. The talk all around him was about how and when to retaliate, but Lev was just Lev, even then. "It's a provocation," he kept saying. "*Uglik* is a provocation." And some people were paying attention to him now. "Don't rise to it. Don't rise." Then he looked up at me and said suddenly, "Can anyone hear my voice?"

Hear it? I said.

"Hear it. Because I can't. I can only hear it from the inside."

Three days later we had the opportunity to study Uglik for a full hour. And even in our world, Venus, even in our world of Siamese twins and mermen and bearded ladies, it was something to see.

We were in the woodshop, which stood in the eternally sunless shadow of its long eave, and we had a clear view of the porch of the infirmary, where Uglik sat with a quilt on a rocking chair, in his greatcoat, his boots. He wore no gloves. Silently we gathered around the window. Uglik's immediate intention, clearly, was to have a smoke—but this was no longer a straightforward matter. Janusz put the cigarette in Uglik's mouth and lit it for him, and then withdrew.

There we were, by the window, six or seven of us, holding our tools. Nobody moved . . . Uglik seemed to be puffing away comfortably enough, but every few seconds he raised one, then the other, bandaged wrist to his mouth before realizing, over and over again, that he had no hands. Eventually, having spat the butt over the rail, it occurred to him, after a while, that he would soon be wanting another. He cuffed the packet onto the floor and kicked it about; he knelt, trying to use his stumped forearms as levers and pincers; then he lay flat on his stomach, and, like a man trying to possess the wooden floor, trying to enter it, trying to kiss it, writhed and rutted about until he snuffled one up with his questing lips.

And of course there was more. Now: to watch a pig bungling a headcount, or indeed a bowl-count or a spoon-count; to watch him pause, frown, and begin again—for a moment it is like a return to school, when you glimpse the absurdity, the secret illegitimacy, of the adult power. It makes you want to laugh. But that's in freedom. It's different, in penal servitude. We stood at the woodshop window. No one laughed. No one spoke and no one moved.

With every appearance of broad satisfaction Uglik returned to the rocker, his head tipped back: the vertical cigarette looked like a piccolo which would now trill Uglik's praises. He patted his pockets and heard (no doubt) the companionable rattle of his matchbox; he reached within. There was an unbearable interlude of perfect stillness before he yelled raggedly for Janusz.

"*I never knew*," we could hear him say, conversationally (and he said it more than once)—"*I never knew it got so cold up here in the Arctic.*"

And as Janusz once again withdrew, Uglik, with a jerk, fleetingly offered him his vanished right hand.

You see, Uglik had something else on his mind: mortal fear. His activities in the women's block, that first night, had resulted in a petition, a demonstration, and now a strike. This would be noticed. And in the end everything certainly added up for Uglik—yes, a most strenuous fate for Comrade Uglik.

We were told the whole story, that spring, by a group of transferees from Kolyma. Recalled to Moscow, Uglik was put on trial and facetiously sentenced to a year in the gold mines of the remotest northeast. He mined no gold, and so earned no food, with the consequence that he became a more or less instant shiteater, and—necessarily—an all-fours shiteater at that. He died of starvation and dementia within a month. Knowledge of this would not have lightened our thoughts and feelings, as we stood watching at the woodshop window.

It was in the nature of camp life that you would suffer even for Uglik—for Uglik, with Uglik. Lev, too, with his gonging head, his left ear already infected and now fizzing with Janusz's peroxide, his inner gyroscopes undulant with nausea and vertigo. We looked on, each one of us, in septic horror. It wasn't just the dreadful symmetry of his wounds—like the result of a barbaric punishment. No. Uglik was showing us how things really stood. This was our master: the man scared so stupid that he kept forgetting he had no hands.

I glanced at Lev. And then, I think, it came upon my brother and me—a suspicion of what this might further mean. I found the suspicion was unentertainable, and I shuddered it off. But I had already heard its whisper, saying . . . The Ugliks, and the sons of the Ugliks, and the reality that produced them: all that would pass. And yet there was something else, something that would never pass, and was only just beginning.

Uglik spat out his second cigarette, wiped his nose on his stump, and shouldered his way inside.

On March 5 we were assembled in the yard and told of the death of the great leader of free human beings everywhere. Silence in the whole zona, a silence of rare quality: I remember listening to the subway noises of the points and wires in my sinuses. It was the silence of vacuum. For at least five or six years, in camp, there had been an intense rumor, daily or even hourly replenished—a rumor that placed Joseph Vissarionovich ever closer to death's door. And what we had, now, was a vacuum. Now he was nowhere. But he used to be everywhere.

From that day on a collision course was mapped out in front of us. No amnesties (not for the politicals), more frequent and more outrageous provocations (more Ugliks), and the uncontrollable impatience of the men—every last man but Lev. So, certainly, we rose up. And the pigs couldn't hold us. It ended on August 4, with Cheka troops, fire engines and steel-plated trucks mounted with machineguns.

We've got a little time, I said. A little time, you and I. And then you're going to have to come out and stand.

Lev was alone in the barracks. He sat at the table by the stove (inactive during the summer month), with his hands folded in front of him like a judge.

"Ah, Spartacus," he said. "*Christ*, what was that? A barricade?"

They were doing the whole zona, sector by sector. The sound of shouts, screams, gunfire, and the collapse of bulldozed walls came and went on the hot wind.

I said, The women are out there. Everyone who can walk is out there, standing in line. Arm in arm. You haven't got a choice. When this is over, do you expect the men to be able to bear the sight of you?

"Mm, the wet stuff. If there *are* any men, when this is over. It wouldn't surprise me if they killed all the pigs, too. A smoke, brother. Yes, go on, a contemplative cigarette . . ."

He had a new voice, now, or a new intonation: precise, almost legalistic, and slightly crazed. A loner's voice.

"You know," he said, "massacres want to happen. They're not neutral. Remember the fascist headcount in the yard in, what, in '50? When the overloaded watchtower collapsed. It was fucking funny, wasn't it? The way it fell—like an elevator cut from its cable. But then we heard the sound of all the rifles cocking. And every man with laughter in his chest, a volcano of laughter. One single titter and it would have happened. The massacre of the laughing men. I knew then that massacres want to happen. Massacres want there to be massacres."

Well, you'd better want a massacre too. And a thorough one.

"Yes, I've already been threatened. It's like a blocking unit in the army, isn't it? Possible death with honor in the van. Or certain death with ignominy in the rear. Smoke up. I've been singing that song, 'Let's Smoke.' "

And there are other reasons, I said. If you sit here on your bench, you're going to feel like shit for the rest of your life.

"Well I won't *not* feel like shit for very long, will I? I've been listening to the radio with Janusz. Things are better in freedom now. The *Doctors* have all been pardoned. 'The flu'—it died when he died. Zoya's not in Birobidzhan. She'll be back in Moscow. In her attic. The future looks bright."

You'll never write another poem. And you'll never fuck your wife.

". . . At last you convince me, brother. I can go out there

and climb on a box and tell them to ignore the provocations and get back to their fucking barracks and wait. Or I can go out there and stand. You know they're going to kill all the leaders. You're about ten times more likely to die than I am. I never realized until now," he said, "that you were so romantic."

Provoked or not provoked, the Norlag Rebellion, I believe, was a thing of heroic beauty. I can't and won't give it up. We were ready to die. I have known war, and it was not like war. Let me spell it out. You are mistaken, my dear, my precious, if you think that in the hours before battle the heart of every man is full of hate. This is the irony and tragedy of it. The sun rises over the plain where two armies stand opposed. And the heart of every man is full of love—love for his own life, all life, any life. Love, not hate. And you can't actually find the hate, which you need to do, until you take your first step into the whirlwind of iron. On August 4 the love was still there, even at the close of the day. It was—it was like God. And not a Russian God. It was magnificent, the way we stood arm in arm. Everyone, the women, Lev, everyone, even the shiteaters, standing arm in arm.

Two days later I was in a filtration camp in the tundra, for resentencing or execution. Semyon and Johnreed had already been shot when the planes arrived from Moscow.

Beria had fallen. The man appointed to arrest him was my marshal, Georgi Zhukov. I love it that that was so. Lavrenti Beria, the clever pervert, looked up from his desk and saw his nemesis: the man who won the Second World War . . . I was meaninglessly transferred to Krasnoyarsk, and barged back up the Yenisei the following spring. At the time of my return a disused dormitory by the side of Mount Schweinsteiger was being rebuilt, to serve as the House of Meetings.

On August 5, 1953, after twenty-eight hours of emergency operations, Janusz looked in the mirror: he thought there must have been some talc in his cap. His hair had gone white.

At around about this time, in another family matter related to the passing of Joseph Vissarionovich, Vadim, my half-brother and Lev's fraternal twin, was beaten to death while suppressing strikes and riots in East Berlin.

5.

"You've Got a Goddamned Paradise in Here"

We thus move on to the conjugal visits. And remember: life was easy, now, in 1956.

The wives had started coming to camp two years earlier, but it was a right granted only to the strongest of strong workers. So that's what Lev became, all over again. Remembering him now, I see a child-sized version of the posters and paintings of an earlier time—the great globes of sweat, the raised veins on the forearms, even the sheet-metal stare that went out to meet the future. He did the work and he earned the right. By now, though, the question went as follows: did he want it? Did anyone?

Considering the variety and intensity of the suffering it almost always caused, I was astounded by how longed-for and pushed-for it remained: the chalet on the hill. I was a close student of this rite of passage—though quite unreflective, I admit, and especially at first. For the husbands, the conjugal visit meant a headshave, a disinfection, a sustained burst from the fire hose. They came out of the bathhouse unrecognizably scoured, stung, alerted, in clothes stiffened not by dirt but by the rasp of ferocious detergents.

Then, with every appearance of appetite and verve, they hastened off, under light guard, to the House of Meetings. And the next day, as each wreck and wraith came stumbling back down the hill, I would find myself thinking: You clamored for it. We fought for it. What's the matter now?

But very soon the meaning of it pressed down on me, and I bowed to the larger power. It really seemed as if this was the goal of the regnant system: it wanted to push every last one of us into the tightest possible corner. "Living in corners" was what they called it in freedom. Four people or four couples or four families per room, living in corners. The women who came to the House of Meetings belonged to a category of their own: they were wives of enemies of the people, and they lived under specific persecution, out in the big zona. And not just the wives but the whole clan. Those airy rooms in the chalet on the hill were in fact very crowded; liquid tentacles of injustice and culpability flowing out from the head of the octopus, and you as its beak.

All the men were different. Or were they? There was a shared theme, I think. And that theme was chronic anemia. They were trying to be red-blooded; and their blood was a watery white. This man's face confesses failure, his body confesses it: the skewed mouth, the cottony weakness of the limbs. This man lays claim to success: he shoves you up against the wall and, in a menacing whisper, looking past you or beyond you, tells you what she did to him and what he did to her. And their hearts, too, were without defenses. This man has just been told that his marriage is over and that his children are now in the care of the state: he will come close to taking the walk to the perimeter. This man seems more or less convincingly buoyed, although he is always thoughtful and often tearful: he is remeasuring and rearranging his losses—and that was probably the best that anyone could hope for. What you were getting was the first wave of the rest of your life. You saw the accumulation of all the complexity that would await you in freedom. Everyone stepped lightly around these men and their mantle of solitude.

You see, the House of Meetings was also and always a house of partings—even in the best possible case. There was a meeting, and there was a parting, and then the years of separation resumed.

Now, whenever work took me up the steep little lane, and I saw the white tiling of the chalet roof, the good white tiling against the black hulk of Mount Schweinsteiger, I felt as I did when I passed the isolator and its double encirclement of barbed wire.

The day came: July 31, 1956. The evening came.

I went to get him in the bathhouse. He stood alone in the changing room, at the far end, on a plank of yellow light. What existed between us now was a kind of codependence. Love, too, but all cross-purposed, and never more so than on this day, this night.

She's here, I said. The Americas is here. They've got her filling out the forms.

He nodded, and richly sighed. It wasn't that likely anymore, but they might have sent Zoya on her way, with a taunt; or they'd give him half an hour with her in the guardhouse, a pig sitting between them and picking his teeth . . . Lev was sheared, deloused, and power-hosed. He was lightly bobbing up and down, like a bantamweight before a fight he expected to win.

We walked, under escort, out of the zona and beyond the wire, over the carpet of wildflowers, and up the steep little lane and the five stone steps to the annex—that compact and manageable dream of gentility and repose, with the curtains, the lampshade, the dinner tray on the backless chair. The thermos of vodka, the candles that in the white night would not be strictly needed. I hadn't sensed much anxiety, until then, in my younger brother. He was young. He was formidably fit. His left ear was dead but no longer infected. He slept on the top tier and ate the full ration plus twenty-five percent.

Then came the flinch: the two inverted chevrons in the middle of the brow, the pleading rictus. It couldn't not be there: fear of failure. Fear of failure, which was perhaps supposed to keep men honest, but turned out to make them mad.

Remember what I told him? You've got a goddamned paradise in here. I also said, Look. Tell me to fuck off and everything if you want, but here's some advice. Don't expect too much. *She* won't. So don't you either.

"I don't think I do expect too much."

We embraced. And as I ducked out I saw the small contraption on the windowsill, the test tube, steadied by its hand-carved wooden frame, and the single stemless bloom—an amorous burgundy.

I have already told you about the evening of July 31.

Count Krzysztov's Coffee Shop. Trying not to laugh, he gave me a cup of hot black muck. Trying not to laugh, I drank it.

Hey Krzysztov, I said. Why do you need all those zeds and the rest of it in the middle of your name? Why not call yourself Krystov?

"No *Krystov*," he said. "Krzysztov!"

There was the lecture on Iran I didn't go to. There was my tryst with Tanya: her notched mouth, like a scar, marking time in what had once been her face. She was twenty-four. Midnight came and midnight went.

The impersonation of reasonable man: that's tiring. The impersonation of someone reasonably good. That's tiring too. I should have slept, of course. But how was I supposed to do that? I had seen a woman who looked like a woman: Zoya, side on, with the whole of her in motion in the white cotton dress, one hand raised to steady the raincoat thrown over her shoulder, the other swinging a crammed straw bag, the Brazilian backside, the Californian breasts, and all of it in syncopation, against the beat, as she moved down the path to the House of Meetings, where Lev stood.

Around me in the dark the prisoners were eating the dream-meal, bolting it, wolfing it. I knew that dream, we all did, with loaves of bread the color of honey or mustard floating past you and turning to mist in your hands, on your lips, on your tongue.

I had something else in my mouth. All night I walked and crawled across a landscape overlaid with grit, a desert where each grain of sand, at some point or other, would have its time between my teeth.

When I first saw him, out beyond the boundary rail, I swear to God I thought he had been blinded in the night. He was being led by the arm, or dragged by the sleeve. Then the pig just swung him out into the yard. Lev turned a full circle, swayed, steadied, and at last began to come forward.

I thought too of his arrival, in the February of 1948, when he had felt his way out of the decontamination shed and moved into the darkness one step at a time—but not slowly, because he knew by then that there were always great distances to cross. Now he moved slowly. Now he was nightblind at noon. As he drew nearer I could tell that it was simpler than that and he just wasn't interested in anything further than an inch from his face. The eyes, rather, were swiveled inward, where they were doing the work of decrease, of internal demotion. Lev came past me. His jaws toiled, as if he was sucking purposefully on a lozenge or a sweet. Some hoarded bonbon, maybe, popped in there, in parting, by Zoya? I thought not. I thought he was trying to rinse out a new taste inside his mouth.

Of course, I had no idea what had passed between them. But I felt the mass of it in a way that went on striking me for some time as tangential and perverse, and uncannily impersonal. It fled without so much as a whimper—all my social hope. More specifically, I ceased to believe, then and there, that human society could ever arrive at something just *a little bit better* than all that had come before. I know you must think that this faith of mine was dismayingly slow to evaporate. But I was young. And for two months in the spring and summer of 1953, even here, I had known utopia, and had quaffed sublimity and love.

For seventy-two hours he lay facedown in his bunk. Not even the guards tried to make him stir. But this couldn't last. On the third morning I waited for the barracks to clear and then I approached. I stood over his curled form. Muttering, murmuring, I rubbed his shoulders until he opened his eyes. I said,

Work today, brother. Food today.

And I peeled him up from the boards and helped him down.

Listen, I said, you can't stay silent forever. What's the worst that could have happened? All right. She's leaving you.

His chin jerked up and I was staring at his nostrils. I don't think Lev knew it until that moment. His stutter was back.

"Leaving me?" he eventually managed to say. And he labored on. "No. She wants to get married again. Properly. She said she'd follow me anywhere. 'Like a dog.' "

Then all is clear, I said. You couldn't do it. Nobody can, not here. You know, in its whole history, I don't think there's ever been a single fuck in the House of Meetings.

"I could do it. Everything worked."

Then tell me.

"I'll tell you before I die." And it took him a long time to get it out. "I have crossed over," he said, fighting it, bringing everything to bear against it, "into the other half of my life."

All that could be done was to help him with his norms and his rations. But he couldn't eat. He tried and he tried and he couldn't eat. He turned his face away. He drank the water, and he could sometimes manage the tea. But nothing solid passed his lips until September. No one joked or smiled or said anything. His attempts to work, to eat, to talk—these were respected in silence by every prisoner.

On the other hand, I too had crossed over into the other half of my life: the better half. He crossed over and I crossed over. We crossed.

By now the camp was simply disappearing all around us. Everything was coming down, and the inmates were mere impediments—we were always getting in the way. As freedom impended, I embraced inactivity. Lev gradually returned to his earlier regime—the jumping-jacks, the lashing skip-rope; he was a boxer again, but with the loath and somnolent look of a man asked to punch far above his weight. We were almost the last to leave. They were practically tearing the rafters off the roof above our heads. And when there was no prison left, they let the prisoners just wander away. Lev went first.

I had three weeks to wait for the rubber stamp. But nothing frightened me or worried me or even bothered me. I minded nothing: the nonappearance of my Certificate of Rehabilitation, the low-priority rail voucher, the "travel ration" of bread. I didn't even mind the train station at Predposylov—at first sight a clear impossibility, with dozens brawling over every seat. I rolled up my sleeves and took my place in the line.

Twenty-four hours later, with caked blood on my cheeks and knuckles, as I settled into my cranny at the carriage window, I turned to see a face pressed up against the glass. I stood up on the bench and hollered through the slit:

How long have you been here?

"Ever since. I want to go back."

Of course you do.

"Not there." He wagged his head. *"There."*

So another fight, another flail through limbs and torsos now unshiftably wedged, and back again, and back again, as I made Lev take my place.

It's all right, it's all right, I kept mechanically shouting. It's all right—he's only little. He's smaller than I am. He's small. It's all right, it's all right.

PART III

1.

September 3, 2004: Predposylov

Today there is a piece in the local paper about the wild dogs of Predposylov.

The writer keeps referring to the dogs as "wild" but his terrified emphasis is on their discipline and esprit de corps. He tells of the "coordinated attacks" they mount on stalls and shops, notably on a butcher's, where they came in through the backyard and "made off" with five meat pies, three chickens, and a string of sausages. The raid, he says, was reconnoitered by the "scout" dog, which barked the all-clear to the "alpha" dog.

Learnedly the writer compares the wild dogs of Predposylov to the "mutant" dogs of Moscow. The Moscow dogs are not called mutants because they have two heads and two tails. They are called mutants because they live in the metro and travel around by train. You may be intrigued to know that I once shared a carriage with a mutant pigeon in the London Tube. It got on at Westminster and it got off at St. James's Park.

An "official source" is claiming that the wild dogs of Predposylov were responsible for the recent savaging of a five-year-old in a municipal playground. There is a picture of the playground—pretty pastels. There is a picture of the five-year-old—comprehensively mauled. Word of the approach of the wild dogs now empties a street, a square.

They tell me, here at the hotel, that the dogs come down the back alley behind the kitchens, every day, at twenty-five past one. The man said you can set your watch by them. I will be taking a closer look at the wild dogs of Predposylov.

Whatever else you may want to say about the place, Dudinka is a perfectly reasonable proposition. If you have timber, and coal, and you're on a big river, then you are going to get something very like Dudinka.

Dudinka has been here for nearly three centuries. Predposylov has been here since 1944. And it's not an aggregation, as Dudinka is, but something slapped down in its entirety—Leninsky Prospect, House of Culture, Drama Theater, Sports Hall, Party Headquarters, and, more recently, Social Historical Museum. Why a city? A mining station, yes, a cluster of factories, quite possibly; and, if you must, a slave-labor camp containing sixty thousand people. But why build a *city* so near the North Pole?

When I got out of Norlag I felt, for nearly a year, that I was treading on the eggshells of freedom. That feeling comes over me here, the unpleasant vibrancy in the shins, the squeamish levitation of the spine. Predposylov is hollow. Underneath the city there are mines a mile deep. The ground itself is a shell you might put your foot through. And there is Mount Schweinsteiger, a black egg in its cup, all emptied out.

This isn't the Second World anymore. It is not even the Third World. It is the Fourth. It is what happens *after*. Already uninhabitable by any sane standard, Predposylov has gone on to become perhaps the dirtiest place on earth. In the hotel there are incredulous environmentalists from Finland, from Japan, from Canada. Yet still the citizens swirl, and the smokestacks of the Kombinat puke proudly on.

I am the oldest man in Predposylov by a margin of thirty-five years.

Late at night I look in on a club called the Sixty Nine (the name refers to the parallel). There is a crooner, Presleyesque (late period), in dramatically swirling white flares. And there are G-stringed waitresses and milling prostitutes and softcore sex films showing on the raised screens. No, I don't feel disgusted. I feel disgusting. People stare at me, as if they've never seen an old man before. Come to think of it, that's probably true: they've never seen an old man before. Other people as old as me, and even older, do exist, don't they, Venus? But really this whole thing has gone on long enough.

My idea is to get my hangover drunk. But I don't go through with it, particularly. My hangover is not a hangover. I was mistaken. It is death. There is something in the center of my brain, something like a trapped sneeze. Which tickles. And the air here makes my eyes sting and weep.

On top of that I now live in a state of permanently lost temper. I lost my temper three days ago and have not recovered it. I am also very voluble, and am already widely feared at the bar here, by the staff and by the customers. Having been silent for so long, I'm now like a very much rowdier version of the Ancient Mariner. The arrangement at the bar is that I do all the buying but I also do all the talking. Sometimes I take a wedge of money from my wallet and burst out of the room looking for someone to yell at.

I've been reading up a bit, and this will be of especial interest to you, Venus, belonging as you do to a generation of self-mutilators. I mean the historical destiny of the urkas.

Now, I have no intention of reopening our debate (let us call it that) on your chin-stud. The soft underbelly of the ear, certainly—but why the chin? I know: it is strangely comforting (you claimed) to focus all your tender feelings on a particular part of your body, now hurt but soon to heal; and thereafter the implanted trinket will mark the spot of your self-inflicted wound. Very well. But what about the "cutting," Venus? I'm assuming you don't do it: your arms, when we meet, are often elegantly sleeveless. But many do. Something like twenty million young Americans, I learn, have regular recourse to the bleed valve.

Urka culture, in its decadent phase, became a lot queerer (the passives cringed, the actives swaggered), making you wonder how crypto-queer it was all along. I feel you flinch. These words are like points of heat on you, aren't they? Your internal censor or commissar—she didn't like that, did she? You have a censor living in your head, but it's not all bad: you also have a beaming cheerleader living there too. So it's not all bad by any means, *having an ideology*, as you do . . . Now understand me, Venus. I hear that the aftermath of a gay love-murder is something to see, but the homosexual impulse is clearly pacific. *Crypto*-queers are supposed heterosexuals; they confine themselves to women; and they are among the most dangerous men alive.

Urka culture, moreover, became self-mutilating, with full urka stringency. They took the battle to their very insides, swallowing nails, ground glass, metal spoons and blades, barbed wire. And this was on top of the self-amputations, self-cannibalizations, self-castrations. My country has always been strangely hospitable to self-neuterers. It began in the eighteenth century, a whole sect of them, the *Castrates*, who held that the removal of the instrument was a precondition, a sine qua non, of salvation.

Cutting. It's done to combat numbness, isn't it? These urkas were convicts, and fought the numbness of prison. Your crowd: what do they fight? If it's the numbness of advanced democracy—I can't sympathize. Other systems, you see, flood the glands and prickle the tips of the nerves.

I had the Social Historical Museum pointed out to me on the way in. It looks like a dry-cleaner's or a Korean takeaway. And it is shuttered, whether for repair, or for final closure, no one knows.

But when I pass it in the early evening the shutter is up. My very small bribe is accepted by a russety youth in white overalls. He says he's an electrician. He convincingly toils, in any event, over a succession of fuseboxes, fixing them, or just stripping them. He rents me one of his three powerful flashlights.

Whose careening beam reveals a short arcade, with four displays on either side—*tableaux morts*. The glass of broken bulbs splits and splinters under my feet as I move forward, past the Voguls, the Entsy, the Ostinks, the Nganasani, and so on: the absorbed or annihilated or alcohol-poisoned peoples of the Arctic. Then I come to the Zeks: us. I look round about me at the other figures, the gaunt revenants of the vanished tribes. The best part of you feels moved to take them as ennobling company, in any form or setting. We were all poor, poor bastards. Still, these were remoter multitudes, and would have succumbed, anyway, to mere modernity.

Their molded shapes stroke the flanks of stuffed reindeers and feed scraps of bread to plastic huskies. I am represented, Lev is represented, by the doll of an old geezer at a low table, before an open stove, beneath snow-furred windows, beside a tousled cot. The Entsy have their reassembled medicine-man outfit, their simulated yurt. We have our foreshortened mittens and our dented metal bowl. All this under the reeling and now failing beam of the flashlight.

"We wanted the best," an old Kremlin hand once said, referring to some other disaster, some other panoramic inferno: "but it turned out as always."

Middle School Number One is like a laboratory and a control experiment. It is showing how you build the Russian totality.

On the third day we reach the point where the situation of the hostages can no longer be plausibly worsened. Consider. They are parched, starved, stifled, filthy, terrified—but there is more. Outside, the putrefying bodies of the people killed on the first day are being eaten by dogs. And if the captives can smell it, if the captives can hear it, the sounds of the carrion dogs of North Ossetia eating their fathers, then all five senses are attended to, and the Russian totality is emplaced. Nothing for it now. Their situation cannot be worsened. Only death can worsen it.

So death comes at the moment of alleviation, of fractional alleviation—because the Russian totality can't assent to that. The medical officials, after negotiation, are dealing with the dogs and the bodies when the bomb falls from the basketball hoop and the roof of the gym comes down. And if you were a killer, then this was your time. It is not given to many—the chance to shoot children in the back as they swerve in their underwear past rotting corpses.

You know, I can't find a Russian who believes it: "We wanted the best, but it turned out as always." I can't find a Russian who believes that. They didn't want the best, or so every Russian believes. They wanted what they got. They wanted the worst.

And now there is a doctor, on the television, who says that some of the surviving children "have no eyes."

Gogol, Dostoevsky, Tolstoy: each of them insisted on a Russian God, a specifically Russian God. The Russian God would not be like the Russian state, but would weep and sing as it scourged.

I am in a terminal panic about my life, Venus; and this is no figure of speech. The panic seems to come . . . Seems? The panic comes, not from inside me, but from out of the earth or the ether. I outwait it—that's all I can do. It rolls by me, and then it's gone, leaving the taste of metal in my mouth and all over my body, as if I had been smelted or galvanized. Then it returns, not the same day, and maybe not the next, but it returns and rolls and billows by me. I think it sweeps the entire planet, and always has. The only people who feel it pass are the dying.

Dead reckoning is a phrase that sailors use—it means the simple calculation of their position at sea. Not by landmarks or the stars. Just direction and distance. I know where I am: the port where I'm heading already shows its outlines through the mist. What I'm doing, now, is dead reckoning. I am making a reckoning with the dead.

There is a letter in my pocket, in my inside breast pocket, which I have yet to read. I keep it there, hoping that it will enter my heart by a process of benign osmosis, one word at a time, on tiptoe. I don't want my eyes, my head, to have to do it.

But I will open it up and spread it out before me, any day now.

2.

Marrying the Mole

Right from the start I have fantasized about the pages that follow. I don't imagine that you'll find them particularly stimulating. But as your nostrils widen and your jaw vibrates, keep an ear out for my clucks of satisfaction—the little snorts and gurglings of near-perfect felicity. This is a "quiet time," such as you could often be prevailed upon to have, when, after too much chocolate and hours of screeching and flailing and whirling, you would submit to a coloring book at the kitchen table or a taped story in your room—before going back to more screeching and flailing and whirling.

I am a stranger in a strange land. A freshly glittering landscape is opening up before me: I mean the mundane. God, what a beautiful sight. There will be ups and downs, of course, especially for your step-uncle and his spouse, but for now these lives rise and fall as they will. We no longer *uninterruptedly* sense the leaden mass, the adenoidal breathing, and the moronic stare of the state. How can I evoke it for you, the impossible glamour of the everyday? We are safe, for now; above us is the boilerplate of banality. Like a saga-spinner of another age, I can almost start the business of tidying up after my guests. "Zoya is as forgetful as ever."

"No, Kitty never did find true love." And this goes on for nearly two whole chapters, and twenty-five years. All is well, all is safe, until we enter the Salang Tunnel.

Before there was that, though, there was this.

As an unrehabilitated political, I was effectively "minus forty," as was Lev. This phrase no longer referred to the temperature in Norlag on an autumn afternoon. For us it now meant that forty cities were out of bounds. We were also ineligible for such perquisites as accommodation and employment . . . I went east from Predposylov, all the way to the Pacific (where I had one swim), before I started coming west. It took me two months to get to Moscow. I spent half an hour with Kitty in a suburban teashop called the Singing Kettle, where a lumpy rucksack changed hands. This was the bequest of my mother, who had died, calmly, said Kitty, in the spring. And then for many months I seemed to be shunted around from berg to berg, always arriving in the small hours—the pale bulb over the station exit, the clockface staring elsewhere, the deep stone of the stairwell. Then you moved off into a blackout and a town of tin. The air itself was ebony, like the denial, the refutation, of the idea of light. A fully achieved cheerlessness, you may think. Darkness, silence, and a palpable rigidity, as if the buildings were seized not to the surface of the world but to its center. And yet I knew that my footsteps made a sound that was no longer feared, and that the huddled houses would open up to me, if not now then tomorrow. Because kindness was rubbing its eyes and reawakening, Russian kindness—the reflexive care for another's good. And I was free and I was sane.

I came equipped with some of my sister's cash, some of my father's clothes, and some of my mother's books—namely, an introduction to advanced electronics, an English primer, and the tragedies of Shakespeare in parallel translation (the main four and also the Roman plays, plus *Timon*, *Troilus*, and *Richard II*). I loved my mother (and she must have scried me here, in minus-forty), as every honest man should and does. And I wondered why it didn't go easier with women and me . . . I was always getting pulled in and moved on, of course, but that year became my nomadic sabbatical—paid leave for travel and study, and for internal relocation. The weight of Zoya, I thought, was also shifting. When I settled down at night she was always there the moment I closed my eyes, waking, half-clad, becomingly disheveled, a slight sneer on her downy upper lips, as she appraised me, her escort to oblivion. But what was the matter with her? Amazingly, and alarmingly (this can't be normal), her effigy, her mockery, had detached itself from the control of my will. In the past, this little mannequin of mine was charmingly rigorous, even draconian in her promptings and insistences. No longer. She was without words and without wants, dumb and numb—unresisting but inert, and almost unwieldably heavy. And her face was always turned away from mine, in illegible sorrow and defeat. I told myself, Well, we're all free now, I suppose. So I would give it up and desist, holding her for a while in my brotherly arms before I too turned away, into sleep and into dreamlessness.

Such sexual kindness that came my way, during that time, and my generally weak response to it, had the curious effect of imbuing me with material ambition. The Slavic form, the oblong of pallor with the marmalade garnish, the grunts of compassion or acceptance, the rustly whispers: this would no longer answer. The center—I could feel it tugging at me, with its women and its money. And in the late summer of 1958 I started orbiting Moscow.

When Lev reached Kazan he found that his wife and mother-in-law had already withdrawn beyond the municipal boundary. He was expected. My sister told me that the three of them were living in "half a hovel" on the outskirts of another city (smaller, more obscure—admissibly abject), where Zoya had found work in the accounts department of a granary. Old Ester made and sold patchwork quilts, and from her sickbed continued to teach Hebrew (a language illegalized in 1918) to an intrepid enthusiast and his three small sons, who drove out twice a week. Lev wasn't doing anything at all. He spent much of the day (according to Zoya's letters to Kitty) in the supine position—understandable and salutary, she said; he was "trying to recover his strength." I said nothing. In his last months there, Lev was again one of the fittest men in Norlag. Deaf in one ear, and with the fingers of his clawlike right hand, even in sleep, locked in the grasp of an imaginary pickax or shovel—but physically strong. He was apparently maintaining that he wouldn't work for the state, which, at this point, wouldn't have him anyway. And the state was all there was. He complained of headaches and nightmares. This was the start of a long decline.

I did better. Living in corners, at first, I poised myself on the northern brink of the capital, and went in every morning on the seven o'clock train. Very soon I had money . . . In 1940 there were four hundred television sets in the USSR. In 1958 there were two and a half million. Every single one of them belonged to a CP. Dealing with the TV sets of the nomenklatura—this was my day job and my night job, installing them, repairing them, or simply clearing up after them, because they frequently exploded (even when they were switched off; even when they weren't plugged in). I would soon indulge in an extravagance: the purchase of my Certificate of Rehabilitation. A considerable expense, in those years, because Russia had not become—or had not yet gone back to being—a bribe society. But I spoiled myself.

When I went away, I was twenty-six. I was getting on for forty when I came back. Gluttony and sloth, as worldly goals, were quietly usurped by avarice and lust, which, together with poetry (yes, poetry), consumed all my free time. I mixed with the black-economy crowd, and my girlfriends were of a type. I suppose it would be accurate to say that they were of the type of the croupier. They were veteran molls and flappers with excellent heads for business. And in my dealings with these women, Venus, I ran into a logistical problem which would trouble me more and more. Take one at random. The inventory of her body and its abilities would, of course, be paralleled by the inventory of her past. And her past would be long, and gruelingly populous. And they were still walking, these men: you see, by that time hardly anybody was getting killed. And I had to know about them. All of them. So I would often find myself prolonging a hopelessly soured romance, sometimes doubling its duration, just to make sure I had winkled out that rugged smuggler from Vladivostok, that sleek bijouterist from Minsk.

Between 1946 and 1957 I ate two apples, one in 1949 and one in 1955. Now I went to however much trouble it took to eat an apple every day. The man who usually sold them to me knew that fresh fruit was something of a delicacy in the Soviet Union. But we had completely different ideas about what an apple was. In the queue there were currents of recognition and mistrust. If the line was fifty Russians long, there would be seven or eight who had been away. There would be another seven or eight who had helped put them there. I would meet the eyes of men and women who agreed with me about what an apple was. I ate everything, the core, the seeds, the stalk.

. . .

What was needed was a meeting. There came a series of second-hand soundings, of vague proposals vaguely deferred. On his side, a sense of reclusion or paralysis; on mine, something like the fear of the diagnostic. The pocket marionette slept beside me, unfrowning in her white petticoat. Would it wake? Would I want it to?

As soon as I got the keys to the new apartment, I made a move. It was an invitation that no Russian could conceivably refuse: a family housewarming at Easter. The time got nearer: the spring equinox, the first full moon over the northern Eurasian plain, the Friday, the Saturday, the Sunday.

I hadn't seen Lev for eighteen months. He came on ahead into the main room, leaving Kitty and Zoya in mid-greeting at the front door. He registered my smile, my parted arms, but continued to review his surroundings—the rugs, the sofas, the chest-high television in its walnut cabinet, the copper horn of the gramophone. A look of mildly amused disdain did not exactly lend charm or distinction to his plinthless, bump-nosed face. I stepped forward and we hugged. Or I hugged. Fuller, softer, and the smell of unlaundered synthetics. But then Zoya was flooding the room with her presence, and there was champagne, and the seven-hour meal began.

"See what I mean?" said Kitty, later. "She's bleeding the life out of him."

Maybe it just looks that way, I said.

It looked that way because Lev kept his good ear (frequently cupped in his clawlike right hand) exclusively trained on Zoya. And she was his interpreter. If you aimed a question at him, he met you with a look of rustic incomprehension, which slowly faded as Zoya, from close range, gave her murmured gloss. He couldn't hear—and he couldn't talk. His stutter was thoroughly reensconced. So it sometimes seemed, when she gestured at him (she always gestured) and raptly mouthed, that this was a rite of lip-reading and sign language, and that without her he would be alone in his mutist universe.

I said, He cheered up a bit later on.

"Yes," said Kitty. "When he was drunk."

She's far more beautiful now, I think.

"Do you think? Yes. She is."

It's got gravitas. She hasn't, but her beauty has.

"I saw you were looking at her . . . Do you *still*?"

No no. Not anymore, thank God.

"Lend him money. Give him money."

But I said I had already tried.

Our reunions, which became fairly regular, soon assumed a pattern—something like a childish feud of assertion and rebuttal. Usually they came to us, but the laws of hospitality demanded that we occasionally went to them. Lev was very different in Kazan. He dominated. We would meet, not at the hotel where Kitty and I put up, but on a street corner in the industrial district—the zinc fogs of Zarechye. There would then be a longish walk, with the visitors falling into step behind the two hooded duffelcoats, the two pairs of squeaking plastic boots. "Ah, *here* we are. How nice," he would say, levering open the sodden door of a hostel canteen or a subsidized cafeteria. While we pushed the food around our plates, he questioned us about its quality. Is the horsemeat accurately cooked? The porridge, I hope, is al dente? When that was over, we'd get a glass of spuddy vodka in some roiling taproom or pothouse. And Lev and Zoya would be squelching back to the bus station at half past eight.

These outings, of course, were clearly, almost openly, punitive. Kitty didn't much mind, and I found it quite funny in a nerve-racking way. It was Zoya who suffered. Fanning herself, she held her head at a prideful angle, taking deep breaths through her rigid nostrils. Her blushes lasted for half an hour, and the great shaft of her throat was like an aquarium of shifting blues and crimsons. In Moscow I naturally retaliated, taking them to modernist black-economy steakhouses, and on to traditionalist black-economy casinos. The tuxed waiter served us green Chartreuse, and I drank to Zoya's thirtieth birthday, raising my chalice under spangleballs and twirling mirrorspheres.

Seeing them together, you couldn't help but be struck by that besetting embarrassment—embarrassing for the Revolution and for all utopian dreams, including yours: human inequality. I hope I have made it clear that I was always rather touched by my brother's physical appearance. "A *face* face," as our mother always called it, though one illumined, in the past, by the smile and the soft blue eyes. And we honor Zoya, don't we, Venus, for her indifference to the norms and quotas of romantic convention—and all that. But there is such a thing as force of life. And the contrast was like something out of a fairy tale or a nursery rhyme or a joke on a seaside postcard.

Jack Spratt would eat no fat. And there was Zoya, seemingly a yard the taller, swinging herself around (this was Moscow) as she laughed, sang, mimicked, brimmed. In those blighted eateries in Kazan, Lev made a big to-do with the bill, intently frowning and shrewdly sniffing over a scrap of paper that said *four dinners*, if that, and suborning Zoya for a strained colloquy about the number of weightless coins to be dropped in the jar. Elsewhere, for every calorie of expended high spirits, Zoya always paid . . . He still wore his hair cropped, prison-style. In the old days, up in camp, I used to like to smooth it back against the nap—it made my fingertips hum. Now, when I once ventured to touch it, the pale fuzz was damp and flat and had lost the power to impart any tingle. He pulled his head away and slid another cigarette into his crumpled mouth.

Over these years there were other changes: significant addenda to the panoply of my brother's attractions. A fold of pudge, very low slung, like a prolapsus or a modern money-belt, between navel and groin; a bald patch, perfectly circular, resembling a beanie of pink suede; and, most mysteriously, an unvarying arc of perspiration, the width of a hatband, running from temple to temple. All three developments looked strangely uniform and standardized on such an asymmetrical little chap. Especially the bald spot. Once, rising suddenly and looking down on him, I believed I saw an open mouth, all tongue, fringed by a beard and a sweat-drenched mustache.

Lev's morose and monotonous asides about my apartment, my clothes, my car (and, during one unrepeated experiment, my croupier) were now like a snore in another room. He didn't despise me, I don't think, for taking the shilling of the state. He despised my appetite. I had drive, and all Russians hate that; but there was a further layer to it. In one of her letters to Kitty, Zoya neutrally mentioned the fact that Lev's circle in the environs of Kazan, such as it was, consisted entirely of elderly failures. If we had been on easier terms I might have said to him that he was feeling what many others felt; he was submitting, in short, to generic emotion. Many others who had been away—they too hated money. Because money was freedom, it was even political freedom, and they had stopped wanting to believe in freedom. Better if no one had it—money, freedom.

I completed his sentences for him, now, when he stuttered. So would you have done. There would have been no end to it if you hadn't. Besides, we always knew, now, exactly where his sentences were going. And he didn't care. He had stopped minding because he had stopped fighting. Lev had surrendered, without conditions, and his stutter had it all its own way; a couple of uppercuts to the chin, and it would leap on his chest and strangle him into silence. Now, when he tipped his head far back, in this or that soup-kitchen in Kazan, it was not to prosecute the civil war with the self—to bring everything to bear. It was in reluctant submission to Zoya's demand that he eat a vegetable. Back went the head; down went the section of blackened beetroot or utterly soundless cucumber. And you had the sense that he wasn't fighting it anymore—he was feeding it. One night, after a great deal of vodka, he told me that he had stopped reading. He said it not casually but with defiance. "If it's bad I don't like it," he went on in a softer voice. "And if it's good I *hate* it."

The girls were more continent, but Lev and I got through the traditional amounts of alcohol. We were both subject to the centuries-old momentum of Russian drunkenness. And it may surprise you to learn that we were good drunks, too, both of us: amenable, reasonably quiet, not likely, on the whole, to brawl or sob. There usually came a point, about halfway through the third bottle, when his eyes met mine and almost confessed to the moment of remission—maybe it was just the nonappearance of the next wave of pain. He didn't draw attention as a drinker. That, I admit, would have been hard to do. But he did draw attention as a smoker. Now, smoking (like drinking) allays anxiety. So try not smoking in Russia and see how far you get. But Lev? He ate with a cigarette in the hand that held the knife. And when he went to stub it out, the movement was but a step on the road to lighting another. He did this all day long. Zoya said he smoked even when he was shaving.

Once, as he inhaled with his customary vehemence, I had

a thought that made my armpits come alive. The thought was this: mad teeth. Those pretty teeth of his, though lavishly stained, still looked sound enough. But the angles had been rearranged. They no longer stood to attention; they leaned and slumped, they crisscrossed. And you do sometimes see this taken much further by the very mad, the teeth tugged and bent by tectonic forces deep beneath the crust.

And me? I think I might have come through all right, if it hadn't been for the dancing.

Three times it happened. Exactly the same thing happened . . . Zoya was superstitiously drawn to the gramophone in my apartment, and would lurk by it and commune with it. Three times she asked with a guilty air for American jazz. She listened, nodding, then with a twist of the head she banged down her glass and extended an elegantly narrowed hand toward her husband. "I don't, anymore," Lev could be relied upon to say. "And you can't." So I danced with Zoya—the exploratory Russified jive. I don't know how good she might have been; what was certain was that it made her madly happy, every inch of her, so much so that you felt implicated and even compromised by the glitter of her ravenous grin. But even at arm's length it was like wielding a woman-sized jumping bean. There was an opposition in her, something like a counterweight in a liftshaft, but ominously misaligned.

Three times it happened: three times she shot out of sight, and there she was at my feet, flat on her back and shaking with silent laughter, her eyes clenched shut and her hands on her heart. The last time (and we have entered a period of last times) her summer dress, resisting the speed of her drop, rode up over her waist . . . And it wasn't just the erotic shock, the power of her two-toned thighs in their stockings, the intricate engineering, and attention to detail, in all those slips and clips and grips. It was the helplessness, the silent laughter, the unseeing eyes, the two hands folded on the heart, it was the helplessness.

"That was the last time," said Lev as I brought her to her feet.

I spoke earlier, I think, of the coldness that is always available to the elder brother. It was this coldness that I now sought. What you're really doing is giving yourself some distance, in preparation for disaster. And—God help me—I had a plan.

Of course, I never asked Lev whether he still wrote poetry. If he had been alive and present, Vadim would have asked him that. Someone who hated him would have asked him that.

As you might put it, Venus: think Thumbelina.

Before her deliverance on the wings of the healed bird, before her redemption at the hands of the tiny Flower King, tiny Thumbelina, you may recall, comes close to marrying the mole. Marrying the dot-eyed insectivore, and spending the rest of her days in darkness.

Could *you* marry a mole? I asked.

"Sure!" you said, with heat.

Sure! I'm not prejudiced! You were six. About a month later, Thumbelina came up again, as the themes of childhood so often do, and I repeated my question. You were silent, troubled: it was your very first dilemma. You had been weighing the reality of marriage to the mole. You now wanted to avoid it. But how could you do that, without hurting the mole's feelings? "It hurt my feelings." Girl children are very quick to recruit that phrase. The only little boy I ever knew well—he would *never* have used it. Girls understand that their feelings also have rights . . . What happened to you, by the way, in the space of those four or five weeks? Some mysterious accession or promotion. If they'd been making a parallel film of your life, they would have known, then, that a new hairstyle or built-up shoes wouldn't do it: the time had come to hire an older actress.

In later life you married the mole, for a while, when you took up with that Nigel. Walking beside you, I said, he looked like your broken umbrella. After him, I noticed, you kept to the flower kings, with only the occasional porcupine or polecat.

But say Thumbelina *had* married the mole. And let's consider it from the mole's point of view. They live together under the soil, in unbreathable damp and darkness. The tiny beauty is a devoted wife. And yet the mole, who can't help being half blind, can't help hating flowers and sunshine, feels the thwartedness of Thumbelina—Thumbelina, who was born from a tulip. It is not in the mole to ask her to go. So he makes his grotto more gravelike, darker, danker, and wills her to leave.

3.

The Salang Tunnel

And leave she did, on October 29, 1962.

It was the day after the defusing of the Cuba Crisis. And this imparted a false perspective. Zoya leaving Lev: that wasn't the end of the world. Not for me, anyway. Was there a precipitant? Kitty herself, who went down there and even cross-questioned the mother, never established the details, though she claimed to sense the aftershock of scandal . . . We knew that Zoya had gone back to her job at the school. Teaching drama. And we knew that she had been summarily dismissed. She was in Petersburg, where old Ester was about to join her. Lev was still in their half of the hovel near Kazan.

I didn't see him for nearly a year. But we wrote. This is what happened to him.

In my first letter I made a practical suggestion. I offered to buy him his Certificate of Rehabilitation, just as I had bought mine some years earlier (and just as I would soon buy my Party card). He took me up on it and asked, in addition, for a large loan, appending a repayment schedule that included calculations for interest. Surveying this schedule, with its percentages, its busy decimals, I felt a cavernous bewilderment. Let's put it that way, for now. The big brother in me was, of course, delighted that Zoya had gone. What bothered me was Lev's response to it: a repayment schedule that ventured far, far into the future. Why *wasn't* it the end of the world?

That October he successfully applied for a job in a mine-construction project in Tyumen, just the other side of the Urals, beyond Yekaterinburg. At Christmas he sent me a photograph of a freckled and bespectacled blonde, standing in a striplit corridor with her hands behind her back. This was the twenty-three-year-old he had met in the works dispensary: little Lidya. I will mention here that in his covering letter my brother confessed to some reactionary pride in the fact that Lidya was—or had been—a virgin. Looking again at the photograph, I had to say that I wasn't at all surprised. I quietly concluded, too, that I wasn't interested in virgins. Naturally I wasn't. What would I do with a virgin? What would we find to talk about all night?

In the new year, in February, he got promoted and she got pregnant. Now, Lev was still a married man, and divorce wasn't as easy as it used to be. Divorce used to be very easy indeed. You didn't even have to go through the rigmarole required of our Muslim brethren, who got divorced by saying "I divorce thee" three times. In the Soviet Union you only had to say it once, on a postcard. But now, for reasons we'll return to, both parties were obliged to attend a court hearing. I couldn't understand why Zoya refused to cooperate, nor could Kitty. Lev felt it prudent to go to Petersburg. As soon as he told her that Lidya was, as the Latins say, *embarazada* (have I got that right?), Zoya complied; and then it was just bureaucracy.

I was best man at the August wedding. My brother seemed much leaner (amazingly, some of his hair had grown back), Lidya's pious parents seemed at last assuaged, and it all went fairly well, considering that Lidya, as Kitty put it, was "out here." Lidya was long and thin, with legs the shape of noodles—another Kitty, another Chile. I found her to be pretty much as far as you could get from Zoya, which is another way of saying that she didn't look very feminine, even as she entered her third trimester. Already the baby dwarfed her. She was like the string on the package. A seven-kilo son, Artem, was duly delivered in November.

Zoya stayed on for a while in Petersburg with her mother. She got involved with the famous Puppet Theater there, making puppet costumes, painting puppet scenery. When the Puppet Theater opened up a subsidiary in Moscow, Zoya was part of the team that came along to run it. In a long, new-broomist letter to Kitty, she said that it was her intention, now, "to return to the life of the heart." She and her mother had their old place back, too. So, once again, Zoya was entertaining in the conical attic.

Kitty called on her, of course. I didn't. I didn't return to the old neighborhood and stand beneath her window. I didn't linger there in all weathers, trying to interpret the movements of shadows on the ceiling of her bedroom. Something else had to happen first. Something that might take a very long time.

Nikita Sergeyevich fell. Leonid Ilich rose.* The Thaw, then the Little Freeze, then the Stagnation.

My lovelife, as I will go on calling it, took an unexpected turn. I was getting older. The croupiers were getting older. They weren't real croupiers—though in my recurring dream about Varvara (the last in the line) she stood over a chip-strewn wheel of fortune, and her rake kept turning into a lorgnette . . . It is hard to get a smile from a good-time girl once she passes the age of forty. Their thoughts are all of solemnization. I tried a couple of younger ones; but with them I always felt that I was on the wrong train or the wrong boat, that the other passengers had different tickets and itineraries, different stamps, different visas. And the whole black-market milieu lost most of its pep after the law of 1961, which gave the economic criminal something new to worry about: capital punishment. So I partly reformed, and joined my generation, entering into a series of more tenacious, more complicated, and (certainly) much cheaper relationships with the children of the Revolution, divorcées, veteran widows, ex-convicts, ex-exiles, all of them fatherless, all of them brotherless. In 1969, on a working trip to Hungary, I met Jocelyn, with whom I more or less cohabited, on and off, until the events of 1982—the Salang Tunnel, and what followed from it.

* Leonid Ilich is Brezhnev, leader of Russia, 1964–82.

By '69 I had found my métier. Robotics, but not yet in its medical applications. To get your hands on materials of international standard, you had to do space or you had to do armaments. Space was oversubscribed, so I did armaments. Rotary launchers for nuclear weapons. That's right, my child: preparations for the third world war. The third world war never became the Third World War, which is just as well. In my current mood, not notable for its leniency, I wouldn't enjoy it—reproaching myself for the Third World War.

I had my own chauffeur-driven Zigli. I shopped in the subterranean valuta arcades. Not very often, about once a year, I would amass a parcel of silk shirts and silk scarves and silk stockings, and scents and unguents and elixirs, and blushers and highlighters and concealers, and send it, without any covering note, to the occupant of the conical attic.

You need to know something about Jocelyn. The main theme of her character was melancholy—melodramatic melancholy. Sad enough in Budapest, Jocelyn was suicidal in Moscow. She carried melancholy around with her, maybe in her handbag, a black and bottomless entanglement of frayed embroidery; or maybe in her hair (another entanglement) it chose to lurk. Her obsession was transience. Oh yes: change and decay in all around she saw. What she feared was the void. Going to sleep was for Jocelyn an existential torment; if she turned in early, you had to rig up a wireless or a gramophone, and she wanted the light on and the door open. The reason for all this, you were led to understand, was the high sensitivity enforced by exceptional intelligence. The more intelligent you were, the more depressed you were bound to get. She could have been the male lead in one of the more forbidding novels of Dostoyevsky. And she was English. Her husband, soon to be estranged, was number two at the British Embassy in Budapest. Jocelyn Patience Harris was a frump and a joke, as well as a door-darkener of mythic power. There were several reasons for the attraction. Chief among them was snobbery.

She was also basically handsome, and rich, and literary, in her way. She never went anywhere without her four or five leather-bound anthologies, or treasuries, of Georgian verse. These we read together. With a new language, of course, the last thing you learn is taste; and for years I would be trying to impress everybody with my marathon memorizations of people like Lascelles Abercrombie and John Drinkwater. At the same stage, my idea of a colloquial English sentence was one that contained lots of phrases like "in the nick of time" and "by hook or by crook." Do you know the expression "a disgusting Anglophile"? That's what I became. And it *was* disgusting. I could sometimes catch myself being disgusting—the tweeds and the twills she imported for me, and the shooting-stick. Also the invidiousness, and the awful pedantry. You yourself got a taste of this when I had that worryingly prolonged laughing fit, and you called Tannenbaum: I had just come across the locution "he had the cheek of taking my photograph" in *Lolita*. Still, I would claim that Anglophilia is not irrational. For this reason. You see, Venus, Russian literature is sometimes thought to be our recompense for a gruesome history. So strong, so real, grown on that mulch of blood and shit. But the English example shows that literature gains no legitimacy from the gruesome. In making claims for world domination, the English novel must look anxiously to the French, the Americans, and, yes, the Russians. But English poetry does not abide our judgment. And it isn't nothing, I contend, to have that history—and a body of verse that fears no man. To have that polity, and that poetry.

Jocelyn, the high priestess of evanescence and infertility, grew impatient, as with a dredged-up irrelevance, when you pointed out that she had five grown daughters and twenty-three grandchildren (each of whom got a card, and a gawky Russian toy, on their birthday). Sexual intercourse, similarly, she regarded as the depth of frivolity, but she would often relent. And then there was the constantly surprising buoyancy of her figure. For some reason her past lovers, including her husband, awoke in me no hostility. To be candid, and therefore ungallant, I couldn't see what they saw in her: *they* were all English already. My inner life, in any event, became increasingly Anglophone. This was part of the plan, too, but it was also a tremendous resource. When Pasternak was silenced as a writer, he turned to translation—of Shakespeare, among others. I know what he meant when he said that he was thereby in communion "with the West, with the historical earth, with the face of the world." Jocelyn wore black, but blackness was what she feared. I dealt with more bilious colors—the browns, the greens.

My nephew Artem still hid from Jocelyn when he was as old as ten or eleven. Then an hour or two later he would creep into the sitting room and stare. And he was not otherwise a timid little boy . . . That didn't stop me taking her down there for a week every summer. Lev and Lidya soon acclimatized themselves. After all, it was not out of the way, in my country, for someone to sit through dinner with their face in their hands; it was not out of the way for someone to seek the fetal position for the duration of a picnic. She would have seemed quite unremarkable if she hadn't been an Englishwoman who could get out any time she liked. Besides, Jocelyn spoke the same amount of Russian as a nineteenth-century aristocrat (perhaps a dozen words), so nobody but me had to listen to her. And I liked to listen to her.

Lev and I once again became close. Ah, these soothing modulations: imagine a whole *life* being told in soothing modulations . . . Lev and I once again became close. We used to sit up late in the kitchen, drinking and smoking. There were several indices of at least partial well-being. The excellence of his chess was one (for me, the achievement of a draw was like clambering onto a raft in a mountainous sea). The stutter was another: he had once again taken up arms. And it no longer felt like a clear unkindness when, one night, I raised the subject of poetry. I was not disinterested. There was something I still very badly needed to know.

That stuff she reads, I said quietly, meaning Jocelyn (you could still hear her radio, next door, where she and I slept), is *terrible*.

"What kind of terrible?"

I explained—pastoral-sentimental, silver-age. I told him about Wilfred Owen, a poet of the First War who started off like that. He had a phrase: "fatuous sunbeams."

That's what all her books should be called, I said. "Fatuous Sunbeams: A Treasury of Georgian Verse." I don't know what she gets out of it.

"Presumably something. Which is better than nothing. Nothing is what I get out of it. It's all dead to me now. You still like it because you never wanted to write it. Poetry."

I waited.

He said, "And I used to think, with Mandelstam, that that was the measure of a man, of a woman: how they responded to poetry. With Mandelstam. It sounds antique now. But maybe I still believe it. And I'll tell you who else believes it. Artem."

Aged fifteen, now, Artem lay hugely asleep upstairs, like a colt, in an Artem-sized bedroom infested with sashes and rosettes.

"I know. I still can't get over it. That I somehow produced such a magnificent creature. *And* he knows his Akhmatova."

For a moment he allowed himself a private smile. Then he sat up straight and said, "When we were away, I still did it. I wrote poems in my head. Right up until '56."

He went still. Our eyes met.

'56, I said. The House of Meetings.

"Oh don't *worry*," he said. "Not now, not yet. But before I die you *will know*."

At this point Lidya entered, yawning and shuffling in her tubular nightcoat; and then Jocelyn entered, unappeasably sleepless, and wearing black. It occurred to me that both these women were Zoya's assiduous opposites, Lidya in the physical sphere, Jocelyn in the spiritual. If you put the three of them in a room together, there would be an $E=mc^2$ event, such as was supposed to happen when antimatter met matter.

Lev, I concluded, was split along similar lines. He was all right now, just about, in his head, but his body was not all right. He had the grated, red-rimmed glance of the chronic. For a while, whenever he had a fit of coughing to get through, he would leave the room; a little later, he was leaving the house. In middle age he was developing "stress" asthma. These attacks involved him in another kind of fight. Back went the head. He could breathe it in but he couldn't expel it. He tried. He couldn't get the air out. He couldn't get it out.

"Stop looking at me like that."

Like what?

"Like the doctors look at me."

Well, God help me, I had a plan.

This period of bourgeois calm, of progress and poetry and upward mobility, of no rape and no murder, is about to close. So let me bring you up to date.

At the turn of the decade we witnessed a series of developments, as if (it now seems) everyone was taking up position, in readiness for November 1982. Lev was hospitalized for a couple of weeks. They wanted to monitor his heart while they soused him in salbutamol, the new asthma drug. Increasingly critical of what she called my "ovine equanimity," Jocelyn went back to England, on a visit. In her only letter, itself a remarkably sunny document, she said that it wasn't the void, and her insight into it, that was depressing her: it was Russia. And she wouldn't be coming back. My nephew, Artem, spent the Christmas of 1980 in the hold of a military stratocruiser, en route to Afghanistan and the war against the mujahideen. He was in the signals corps, and would be some way back from the front line. Christmas, an anniversary of no significance to Muslims or to Communists. And Zoya—Zoya did something strange.

News of her always came to me, with a glint, through the prism of my sister. The two of them met up about once a month, and when Kitty gave her reports she assumed the air of a hard-pressed social worker describing a particularly obstinate case. On the other hand, she was liable, as she spoke, to sudden physical expansions; for minutes on end she lost her slenderness, her meagerness, and swelled with possibilities . . . Often reaching for her inverted commas, Kitty had me know, for instance, that Zoya had "fallen in love with 'a wonderful choreographer,'" that Zoya had been "swept off her feet by 'a marvelous costume-designer.'" Over the years her menfriends seemed to decline in both caliber and staying power. I prepared myself for the era of the wonderful prop-shifter, the marvelous ticket-puncher, and so on. But as the old decade turned into the new, two things happened, and Zoya changed. She turned fifty-three and buried her mother in the course of the same week. And Zoya changed. Early in 1981 she told Kitty, very quietly, that she had accepted a proposal of marriage.

Go on then, I said. Who to?

Kitty paused, prolonging her power. Then she said, "Ananias."

No. I thought he was dead.

"Ananias! How can we possibly tell Lev?"

Only the one name: Ananias. Now an occasional contributor to the Moscow wing of the Puppet Theater, Ananias was the formerly famous dramatist. *The Rogues*, the play that made his reputation (there were also stories and novels), came out in the mid-1930s. It was set in a corrective-labor camp, and was about a group of mildly feckless urkas. In the early 1950s it was revived, and then rewritten by him for the cinema, very successfully, and with a different title—*The Scallywags*. Ananias was eighty-one.

And Kitty? We had better round off Kitty, because we are not going to be seeing much more of her. No, she never did find true love. The passion was not a strong one, but it led to her incurable attachment to a married man. He had long ago stopped promising to leave home. Later, she additionally befriended the wife, and became a kind of Aunt Phyllis to the only child. I tell you this just to show that people everywhere can create their own deadfalls, their own adhesions. It doesn't always need the orchestration of the state.

At this time, after Jocelyn, I was having a restful romance with one of the interpreters at the Ministry of Defense. Restful, because timid Tamara was still in mourning for her husband of twenty-five years (and her prior history was the work of a single shift). Although her colloquial English was only middling, her technical English was first-rate, and I would be needing that. Tamara was slightly insane too, but tending the other way, and more dreamy than manic. Her obsession was her dacha—the converted beach hut in southern Ukraine on the shores of the Black Sea. She vowed to take me there in the spring. As I went off to sleep, she spoke to me in furry whispers. In that simple shack we would dwell, swimming naked each morning in the turquoise waters, and we would walk for hours along the sand under the confetti of white butterflies. I do love to swim, it's true, to pound around and then float and wallow, unsupported, without connection . . .

On November 3, 1982, along with hundreds of others, Russian and Afghan, Artem was killed in the Salang Tunnel on the road heading north from Kabul. The Salang Tunnel, the highest on earth, which bores through the Hindu Kush, was Soviet-built (in 1963), and was therefore, and remains, a four-dimensional, 360-degree deathtrap, even in peacetime. Artem's convoy, having cleared one avalanche, was heading north. Another convoy, two miles away at the far end, having cleared another avalanche, was heading south. There was perhaps a collision; there was certainly an explosion.

We were told that "several dozen" died, but the figure was probably closer to a thousand. It wasn't the blast that killed them. It was the smoke. Because the Russian authorities wrongly believed that Artem's convoy was under attack from the mujahideen. So they sealed the Salang Tunnel at both ends. And why do that *anyway*? Blinded, maddened, choking, groping, flailing, pounding—and slow. A total death, a *deep* death for Artem.

I got to the house on the day after the telegram. All the blinds were drawn. You may wonder how I had the leisure to do it, but I thought of Wilfred Owen: "And each slow dusk a drawing-down of blinds." He was picturing a bereaved household (or a near-infinite series of such households) in the "sad shires"—October 1917. The drawn blind was an acknowledgment and a kind of signal. But the stricken need the dark. Light is life and is unbearable to them—as are voices, birdsong, the sound of purposeful footsteps. And they are themselves ghosts, and seek an atmosphere forgiving of ghosts, and conducive to the visits of other ghosts, or of one particular ghost.

For as long as I could bear it I sat with them in the shadows. Ten minutes. In the station hotel the water in the bathroom ran black. And this didn't in the least surprise me or concern me. What color was water supposed to be? I looked in the mirror and I felt I could just remove it, my face. There would be clasps, behind the ears, and it would come away . . . I telephoned every few hours. I went over. And each time I came out of the front door—it was like fighting your way through the fathoms and snatching the first mouthful of air.

He said this to me. This is all he said. He said, "The worst is how much I pity him."

Lidya, now, was always upstairs, in his room.

I said softly, What's she doing up there?

"So young, and so afraid. She's up there smelling his clothes . . ."

The blinds—they never did go back up. On the third morning Lev said that, insofar as he could locate his physical being, he seemed to be suffering from vertigo. He was admitted to the infirmary in Tyumen and transferred that afternoon to the hospital in Yekaterinburg. Detaching me from Lidya's side, the doctor said that he had never seen a patient respond so weakly to such a massive infusion of drugs. He called it "a failure cascade": organ after organ was closing down. My brother lay still and silent on the raised bed, but he was also in rapid motion. He was spinning around my head. He was disappearing into a maelstrom.

And conscious, all the way. His eyes swiveled from face to face—Lidya's, Kitty's, mine. His eyes were the eyes of a man who fears he has forgotten something. Then he remembered. He said goodbye to us in turn. He seemed to consider my face. Don't expose me, I thought. Don't tell.

"At last, no?" he said. And then the word "Please."

Lev died on the same day that Leonid Ilich died—November 10. On the same day as the man who sent Artem into the Salang Tunnel.

4.

The House of Ill Fame

She was living, Venus, in a house of ill fame . . . Wait. What about a decent interval? No, we have already *had* a decent interval. It lasted for twenty years. Of course, I could tell myself, as I walked through the streets of the capital, that I was a messenger, bearing mortal tidings, like the best of brothers—the best of brothers. But I didn't do that. I had a plan. And she was living, Venus, in a house of ill fame.

It was the landmark mansion block on the Embankment, looming square of shoulder, its bemedaled chest out-thrust, as if standing to attention over the Moscow River: neoclassical Gothic, and violently vast. When I call it infamous, which I do, I am using the word in its older sense, and not just as a synonym for *notorious*. They put it up just after the war, to house the victorious nomenklatura; and it still contained many a venerable and contented mass-murderer—taciturn amnesiacs on state pensions. The residents were by now more diversified, but as I entered, and registered, and waited while the guard made his call, I could have come across a Kaganovich here, a Molotov there.* I stepped into the wooden lift, which swilled on its tumblers. When it rose, the old contraption began to screech, as if the shaft with its swooning counterweight was an instrument of torture eight floors high. The encaged platform was being drawn up into it, into the house of infamy.

I had walked across town from the Rossiya, where I had taken a suite overlooking Red Square. November 17, 1982, and Leonid Ilich was being laid to rest. At the funeral of Joseph Vissarionovich, in 1953, the whole city was ascreech—human howls, the horns of cars and trucks, the factory whistles, the sirens. In her entire history, Venus, Russia was never madder than on that day. Hundreds, perhaps thousands, were trampled or crushed (and not just in Moscow). My sister was there. Corpses, she said, rolled like barrels down the sharp incline into Trubnaya Square and jolted to a halt in a pond of blood. Even Pasternak, even Sakharov, felt the panic. An outrageously vast presence had disappeared; an outrageously vast absence took its place. In the vacuum everyone seriously believed that Russia itself would—would what? That Russia would stop existing. Only the Jews

* Lazar Kaganovich and Vyacheslav Molotov belonged to the regnant inner circle from the mid-1920s to the mid-1950s. Both were key actors in the two great waves of terror, 1931–33 (the countryside), and 1937–38 (the cities and towns). This is the last footnote. And the reader may want a question answered, in view of what is to come. Do I forgive him? In the end, yes, I do. The only thing I don't forgive is that he wouldn't let me drive him to the airport. That was *O'Hare:* at least another hour.

were glad. Only the Jews and the slaves . . . No grief, no apocalypse, for Leonid Ilich. Not a lethal superfluity of human beings but, instead, an embarrassing dearth. Mourners had been trucked and bussed in for the day from outlying farms and factories. They wore black. The blacks of the women frayed and puffy, the blacks of the men lucent with use. I walked through a city of Jocelyns and undertakers. I too wore a black tie, beneath my white silk scarf, my cashmere overcoat.

These last items I surrendered to the uniformed maid. Then I turned. Zoya stood at a round table, leaning back on it with her gloved fingertips. She, also, was in mourning wear: a black suit, black stockings and shoes, and a fine-meshed veil attached to the rim of her velvet hat.

"Cleopatra," she said in an unamused voice, "had the right idea." She looked at me consideringly—my frown, my knitted black tie. "She killed the messenger if he gave her bad news, of course. Quite properly. But sometimes she killed the messenger before he said anything at all. Before. I ought to kill you now. Kitty told me about Artem. But this isn't about him, is it? It's about his father. Your brother. My first husband."

And she swayed forward and engulfed me. It was my intention, whatever happened, to load up on sense impressions, future memories of smell and touch. And Russian men are old hands at comforting bereaved Russian women. They know that the embrace will last a long time, and that a certain license obtains. It seems to be permitted to stroke the sides of the upper thorax; and when you murmur "there there" you are also referring to the pendency beneath one armpit, the pendency under the other . . . Zoya cried with her whole body. I felt her hot breath in my ear as she heaved and gulped and popped, and her veil grew moist against my cheek. The veil—somber hosiery for the eyes, the nose, the mouth; when she straightened up and backed away it was stuck flat to her face, and not just with tears but with other fluids. She held up a black hand and pointed with the other.

In the sitting room one of the three leaded windows was open to the morning. As I approached the wavering bank of glass I picked up an odor, sweet but sinisterly sweet; it came, I knew, from the Red October Chocolate Factory across the way, but it reminded me of the smell of humanity in the Arctic thaw. Abruptly the maid's uniform moved past me and she shut the window with a soft exclamation of surprise. How, she then asked, did I like my coffee? I declined. I feared even the slightest upsurge of agitation. You should take note of this. I cannot talk about the loss of a child. But the loss of almost anyone else is a kind of intoxicant. Mine was a rare and dreadful case, I agree, but I suspect that the invigoration is universal. You are being asked, after all, to register the greatest of all conceivable contrasts. And I was very alive. Don't worry. The bill, on its silver tray, is presented later. Your payments are made on the installment plan—what the English, artistically but without truth, used to call the never-never. As I say, you should take note of these thoughts on bereavement, Venus. You who are about to be bereaved.

I was on my fourth cigarette by the time she again appeared. The veil was lifted now, pinned to the hat . . . At reunions after long intervals, beautiful women do this, I have found—they sidle toward you with their faces lowered and at an angle, peeping out, not from the ruins, but from the museum of what they once were, now that their trophies are kept behind glass. Zoya, her own curatress. And there of course it all was, despite her coloring of dusk and blush, her self-moisturizing flesh: the silky fissures of the forehead, the bruised pouches beneath the orbits, the nicks on the upper lip, and the extra painlines that all Russians have, stressing the push of the jaw. Seen head-on, her figure looked to have kept its contours and outline, but when she turned, it was as if (to persist with the schoolboy metaphor) a reeflike Caribbean island had unmoored itself and drifted all the way to the Gulf of Panama.

"His suit," she said. "His shoes! I felt your overcoat for five whole minutes. I didn't stint myself."

And you, I said. Your hair . . .

"It's still black. That's because I dye the shit out of it once a week. Oh, I'm gray. Like Voltaire. It's awful, presenting yourself to the past. I want all my old friends to be struck *blind*. I—" She dropped her head and made a listening face. She said, "He's coming. He's coming. He'll only stay a minute. He wants to pay his respects."

And in he came, through the double doors . . . As late as

1960 or so, it was possible in Moscow and Petersburg to see Ananias on posters and billboards. Sitting at a table, chin on palm, the toppled quiff of brown hair, the mock-resolute pout, the air of bohemian entitlement. And now? It is the fate of a significant fraction of little old women to turn into little old men: little old men in knickers and camisoles. You don't so often see the process going the other way, but here was Ananias, a little old bag in a suit and tie. A little old boiler in gartered socks and black brogues. Even the stiff, tugged-back shoulders were feminine. He also had that spryness which, in elderly ladies, some claim to admire. Only in the brambly eyebrows did you see the burdens and calculations of the male.

Zoya introduced us. And you'll think I'm making this up, but I'm not. His handshake was so disgusting that I at once resolved to hug him or even kiss him, in parting, rather than shake that hand again. White and humid, the flesh seemed about to give, to deliquesce. It was like holding a greased rubber glove half full of tepid water.

At this point Zoya excused herself, promising her anxiously peering husband a swift return.

Ananias settled in his chair, saying, "I'm afraid you must have had a shocking flight over the mountains."

I said, The mountains? No. They're hardly worth the name of mountains.

"Ah, but the air pockets, do you see, the low pressure. You get it there because . . ."

As we talked, I found myself in the process of understanding something about Ananias: a pretty exact calculation could be made. The previous year I had seen a rerun of the film they made of his play, *The Scallywags*. I had also looked at a collection of his short fiction, published in 1937. This book greatly surprised and disquieted me. On the face of it his stories followed the social-realist pattern: say, the vicissitudes of a pig-iron factory or a collective farm, leading to a strengthened affirmation of "the general line." Here was the anomaly: Ananias had talent. A consistently high level of perception was still alive and writhing. The prose lived. And when you came to the bits where he had to do the formulas and the piety—you could almost see the typewriter keys getting seized and wedged together like a mouthful of spindly black teeth. In the 1930s a talented writer who wasn't already in prison had just two possible futures: silence, or collaboration followed by suicide. Only the talentless could collaborate and stay sane. So Ananias was a much rarer being. Within minutes I could feel the force of his accumulated mental distress, as unignorable as the touch of his hand or the smell of his breath. His breath, like the air above Predposylov.

She always seemed to be coming and going, and now she was coming again (her neck erect, like her harnessed gait). Ananias looked at her as if for leave and said in his weightless voice, "I commiserate with you in your tragedy. And the boy. Horrible. Horrible! An only child," he said, nodding to himself. "This war is acting on us like a poison. The numbers are not yet enormous. But the young men being killed have no brothers, no sisters. Their families are at a stroke destroyed. Our whole society is cringing from this war."

He paused, and his chin dropped onto his chest. When his gaze came up again, you saw that even the glass of the eyes gets old, ridged with scoopings and hardnesses. He said, "I'm as old as the century. Older! 1899!" His head twitched. "And your brother was still a young man. What was he, my dear? The same as you, no? Younger. A mere calf. And to give up the ghost like that. At *his* age. Quite extraordinary. *Quite* extraordinary."

Ananias sat with his hands on his lap, their fingers interjoined. His hands—how could they bear each other's touch? Why didn't they fly apart? And I felt an abstract pity for the mote of dust that might be caught in there, in the vile bivalve of his clasp. The answer I gave was valiantly mild, but it had already become clear that there would be no second handshake to avoid or survive.

I said, I assume you know that Lev spent ten years in camp.

"There was no other way, do you see. Free men would not have done that work, the mining for gold, for uranium, for nickel, all things the nation needed for its very survival."

It was after the war, I said. We went there after the war.

"The institution got stuck. As institutions do. But that was all a very long time ago. And look at *you*. You've made your peace with the state. And doing *rather* well out of it, thank you very much. It hasn't done you much harm, has it?"

I waited. I looked at Zoya, expecting a glance of warning. But her head was down. It seemed to me that every Russian was always doing the same thing. We were always fighting off an insanity of bitterness. For the moment I confined myself to saying that the reality of the camps was not what he chose to describe.

"Chose? Chose? I didn't choose. You didn't choose. *She* didn't choose! *No one chose.*"

And I said it. I said, You chose. And you know who you're like? You're like the men and women in camp—the men and women who aren't men and aren't women. They had it taken away from them. But you. You did it all by yourself.

Time ticked past. And then he slapped down his hands on the leather arms of the chair and tried to rise. In a voice grown suddenly lost and childish he said, "Oh, why do people think they can come back and upset everyone? They think they can just come back. And cause such pain with these old wounds."

Zoya helped him up. She gave me a nod and a quelling gesture, and guided Ananias toward the door, leaving me with the onerous notion that she was going off to attend to old Ester.

I spent this second intermission in a tour of the room; and it seemed that every ornament and gewgaw, every cornice and curlicue, had been potentiated, if not directly financed, by the forgiving laughter Ananias had provoked, nationwide, with his scapegrace brigands, stumbling just a little bit on their path to redemption. In *The Rogues* (1935) the fascists, the politicals, were straightforwardly demonic; in *The Scallywags* (1952) the politicals were demonic—and Semitic: we were all fagins and shylocks, we were all judases. Over in the corner there was a little shrine to Ananias's more signal successes—autographed photos, cups and sashes, the certificate confirming his status as a Hero of Socialist Labor . . . I was also considering the depth of Zoya's failure: her failure to live by the heart. I myself knew what a dispiriting project that was, with my widows, my orphans, the middle-aged waifs and changelings, the mice and the guinea pigs still rattling around the abandoned lab, long after the experiment was over. And now expected to just live out their lives.

Again she reentered. Jewess, I whispered. And "Ananias"—wasn't that Jewish too? Oh, what's *wrong* with Russians about the Jews . . . She closed the double doors and sank back with her hands flat against the teak. Now she moved forward with something that resembled the comic slovenliness of her old walk, and when she dropped herself onto the sofa her feet momentarily rode up from the parquet before resettling themselves as she patted for me to join her.

"He's all right."

You could feel her sigh through the sofa's frame.

She said, "We've got about five minutes. Then he'll start. It's good of you to come but it hurts to see you. And it hurts to be seen. Why are you here? You must have a reason. Knowing you."

I said I had two. Two questions.

"Begin."

I asked her what happened in the House of Meetings.

"The house . . . ?" In her brow many tiny lines conspired

before she said, "Oh. Then. Why do you ask? Nothing happened. I mean, what do you think happened? It was lovely." Seeing my surprise, and surprised by it, she said, "I suppose it was all too much, in a way. Lots of tears, lots of talk. As well as the obvious."

I then apologized in advance for my unattractive haste, adding not very truthfully that certain plans of mine were impossible to postpone. I said I was getting out: America. Where I would be rich and free. I said I had thought about her a thousand times a day for thirty-six years. Here and now, I said, she delighted all my senses.

So the second question is—will you come with me?

There it was again: the sweet smell. But now all the windows were closed. And at that moment, as the blood rose through my throat, both my ears gulped shut, and when she spoke it was like listening long-distance, with pause, hum, echo.

"America? No. I'm touched, but no. And if you want me to just kiss goodbye to what I have here and put myself back at risk, at my age, you're wrong . . . America. It's months since I've been out in the street. It's months since I've been *downstairs*. I'm far too drunk. Can't you tell?"

I would have gone on but Ananias was calling her name and she said, "I'm so finished. Anyway. Not *you*. Never you. Him. Him."

All the saloons and bistros were shut to the lunchtime trade, out of respect. Respect for the most decorated man in

Russian history, respect for the seasoned leader who, on his public appearances, had been drooling all over himself for at least five years. At a resilient pace I had crossed the Big Stone Bridge, with echoing footsteps. You will be wondering at my tone, Venus, wondering at my resilient pace, my echoing footsteps . . .

I bought my way into one of the clubs I used to go to in my black-economy days. More Party people now, it seemed, as well as the usual crowd of skivers and chancers. I took a stool at the bar and ordered a glass of champagne. The TV set, mounted on a wall of booze, was soundlessly screening the state funeral. And it looked like the usual masterpiece of boredom—until something happened. Something that silenced the room and then ignited it in a crossfire of wolf whistles and catcalls. The soldiers of the honor guard were about to close the coffin; Leonid Ilich's widow, Viktoriya, took a lungful of air and paused. And then she committed a criminal act. She made the sign of the cross. There was only one human being in my country who could have done that without reprisal: her. She made the sign of the cross over the dead emperor of the godless.

And did I have hopes of resurrection, of resurrection at the eleventh hour? I have to say that I did; and not, in my case, without some reason. I was taking my leave of the house of ill fame—and it wasn't a good exit, Venus. I was all right at first, but it wasn't a good exit. Zoya unlocked the tall door, and I moved past her and turned with my scarf and overcoat in my arms. She offered me her black satin hand, knuckle-up. Which I did not take. Ananias was calling her name. That was the accompaniment to my valediction: Ananias's ever less frequent but increasingly desperate cries.

I said in a raised voice that she could not possibly be living with less honor than she was now. Considering what had happened to Lev. And to me and the other twenty million. There was more, there was too much, in this vein. Then came the moment when I referred to her husband, with clearly superfluous asperity, as a rancid old dyke. Zoya gave a jolt of the shoulder. I waited for the door to be swung shut in my face. But she didn't do that; her body changed its mind, and she stepped forward and leaned against me and kissed my lower lip, holding it between her teeth for a second and looking at my eyes.

This was a test.

Now you must believe how passionately, how tumultuously I wish that that had been the end of it, and that she had never come to my rooms at the Rossiya.

5.

Blood on the Ice

One of things I loved about your mother was her name. The name is of course very pretty in itself, but it was also, I thought, an evocation of the shape of her life, with its cyclical resurrections: the sharecropper childhood, the cages of New Orleans, the convenient first marriage, the factory years, the time with your father, all of it survived and surmounted. And then you, the late arrival, the "autumn crocus." And then her time with me. But I, I did not have the power to rise from my ashes. When I met your mother I was threatened in the deepest sources of my being. Your mother got me through that—or past it. But I could not do what the firebird does and reascend in flames.

You were impressively and dauntingly distressed when I told you, soon after her death, that our marriage had been chaste. You were seventeen. I should have kept my mouth shut. If she didn't tell you, why should I? My thoughtlessness, I would like to claim, was a consequence of my crude euphoria: it was the day you decided not to go and live with your aunt, uncle, and cousins, as we had more or less intended, but to stay on with me. The sense that Phoenix, in her final span, remained imperfectly fulfilled: this is what hurt you. All I can do is repeat, with all possible diffidence, that your mother didn't want for spoonings and cuddlings and cradlings.

And if it still hurts you, Venus, then now at least you will understand.

When I opened the door to her I felt like a child who believes itself lost on a swarming street and then suddenly sees that all-solving outline, that indispensable displacement of air.

She had a blond fur coat over one shoulder. And a transparent polythene pouch held to her chest: gumboots. I looked down and saw her oxblood high heels and the bands of wet on the shins of her stockings. Her Turkic face was as pale as a plaster cast—outside nature. I was reminded of the yogurty unguent that Varvara, my final croupier, used to entomb herself in, nightly, toward the end; it changed the color of her teeth—from almond flesh to an almond's woody husk.

In Zoya swayed, throwing her things (including, I now saw, a Davy Crockett fur hat) the considerable distance to one of the heavy armchairs. I asked her what she would like—vodka, champagne, perhaps a warming cognac? She declined with a shooing flutter of both hands.

"I told them you were my husband," she said. Then she dug her fists into her hips and leaned forward, like a schoolgirl sending a taunt across a playground. "Don't think I've changed my mind. I'm not going anywhere with you—but I *am* going to change my life."

The room had a dining table in it: four cylindrical straw stools, a circular silver tray with glasses, a bottle of mineral water, a decanter of British malt. Here she established herself. With impatient, with already exasperated fingernails she picked at the cellophane of a cigarette packet, holding it very close to her eyes.

You're dry, I said.

"Dry." The low stool creaked beneath her. "Also on my own, for now. My only friend is the maid. He's in the clinic for his checkup. They do him bit by bit. And it's everyone *else* who dies . . . You're right. I hate me. I hate me. And I want to say sorry to you. If you were being truthful then I'm sorry. I bet you think you're quite a plum, compared to him. But look at you. Look at your eyes. You're not kind. And I don't have a choice: I must be with the kind. Ooh, I know you'd find a way to torture me. And anyway you're Lev's *brother*. So sorry again, mate. There isn't much in this for you, I'm afraid. If Kitty was back I'd go to her. I need to talk about Lev. Will you listen for an hour? And then we can say goodbye as brother and sister."

At this point, you may be surprised to hear, my heart was like a hive of bees, and my ears, again, were thickly clogged; both conditions would pass. Her words make perfect sense to me, now. They made no sense to me then. Zoya said she needed to talk, but I was basking in the assurance that she had come to my rooms for quite another purpose. She might, at most, have a scruple or two she would want me to help her out of. Just as I would help her out of her clothes. The decision, I imagined, had already been made. This morning.

Yesterday. And that decision would beget another decision. Because everything would look very different to her, after a night at my hands.

I was of course prepared for a longish interlude of volubility. Giving myself small doses of the boggy, peaty scotch, I listened and I looked. She wore a close-fitting business suit of charcoal gray, and a plain blue shirt of manly cut. It was three o'clock in the afternoon. Through the far window you could see the dusk as it gathered over Red Square—Red Square, and the Asiatic frenzy of the Kremlin. The straw stool crackled under her shifting weight.

Zoya's time with Lev, she told me, before he went away, was "like a new universe," because at last she had found someone "just like me." Someone who didn't hold back. In matters of the heart "he always said I was hopeless. Far, far too total." But what he didn't yet know was that even in her wildest infatuations and most reckless surrenders she was *still* holding back. "I mean physically too," she stipulated, nodding. With Lev she did not hold back. And my brother (it became clear) was equal to it . . . So. Lev, the "shock" lover, the sexual Stakhanovite, with his hundred tons of coal. I absorbed this in perfect calm. A premonition of what must now follow was twining itself through me; but Lev I forgave. He was among the dead. He was forgiven. And the living? In all my thoughts of Zoya, I had never looked beyond the opening act. And now the opening act was at last secure. So I looked and I saw.

"When he came back, things were in general very hard. As you know. And he made a bit of a show of being grim. But when it was just him and me, alone, it was still heavenly. He wondered how I could get up in the morning and go to work, but for me it was like fuel . . . You know, Lev cried in his sleep. Not every night. It was always the same dream, he said. Something that had happened in camp. He didn't want to talk about it but I pressed him. He said he kept dreaming of the guard with no hands. No hands. As if they'd just been lopped off in Saudi Arabia. Unspeakable. But why would that make you cry? And so wretchedly."

And for a moment she cried herself, in silence; her eyes shed a tear each. She resumed, saying, "Five more years. I still don't understand what happened. I mean I do and I don't. That last summer he became very withdrawn. He was not well physically, I think. He turned away from me. At night he turned away. And the words. They went too. It all went. So then I did something stupid. The whole time he was gone I never looked at another man. It wasn't will. My eyes just didn't look. I was him and he was me. And when he turned away from me I became very confused. Actually I was desperate. If I'd been a peasant in a time of hunger, I'd have skipped all the mice and the berries and the bugs. I'd have been thinking about cannibalism *straight away* . . . There was a young teacher, a colleague. And a complete brute, as it happened. I couldn't even keep the thing secret. The whole school found out. Then it was over. I thought it might not be. Sometimes there is—forgiveness. But it was over. And then he knocked up that bitch in Yekaterinburg."

Here they come again, I was vaguely thinking—the brutes and the bitches. Here they come. I said, She wasn't a bitch.

"Of course she wasn't a bitch. It's just a way of talking. Anyway. And after that, God. Man after man after man after man after man."

Something in the room had begun to change. This was what is called a nodal moment—a moment when timelines fork and branch. Over the last half hour I had acclimatized myself to Zoya's snow-white brow, her habit of jerking her head as if to evade a vindictive housefly, the way she crushed her hands between her knees to control them or just to know where they were. Her pallor: the flesh had the numb glisten of white chocolate—but with the promise of other tints in it, yellow, beige, brown, rose. Now in a single pulse Zoya's body went still and all her color returned. All her dusk and blush. She stood. She looked at the floor and said in a voice that had gone an octave deeper,

"My clothes are too tight. Where's the bathroom?"

Through the bedroom, I said—the sliding door.

And even as her thighs swished past me I was contemplating, with a blood-rush all my own, the enormous project that lay before me. There was a gigantomanic headiness in the appraisal of its dimensions; I might have been looking at a blueprint of the White Sea Canal or the TransArctic Railway. And what was this enterprise? Zoya's past—Zoya's men. Not Lev, but every last one of the others. Even the slug trail of Ananias. Oh, what work lay ahead of us, what prodigies of retrieval and categorization, what audits and manifests, what negations, what cancellations . . .

"This is pathetic, but I think I need a doctor."

I turned. She stood in the doorway, jacketless, shoeless, her color further freshened by the lightest coating of sweat. Her skirt was loosened at the waist: an inverted triangle of white against the charcoal gray . . . For some time, perhaps right from the start, I had been intermittently conscious of a drift or division inside me; and as I came up off the chair I had the sense that I was leaving another self, another me, still sitting quietly at the table.

But I came up off the chair saying no no no no no, it'll pass, it'll pass, you just, here (you're on *fire*), that's it, I've got you, off with this now, good girl, and with this, lift your foot, and the other, there we are, there we are. There there. There there.

She stood above me, a towering ghost in a white petticoat.

"Out of the way. Off with you. Out! Just the sheets," she said. And she slid in between them.

At the dining table I drank a glass of whisky, and smoked a cigarette. I made a call to the hotel operator. When I returned to the doorway I saw that she had thrown off the upper sheet and now lay with her right arm under the pillow. One leg was straightened, the other fully flexed. A leaping dancer, frozen in midair.

Many times in the past, like all Russian men, I had found myself paying court to a woman who was, by any reckoning, helplessly drunk. No false delicacy, then, could deter me from paying court to a woman who was in withdrawal. First, I shed some clothes, attaining rough parity with my guest; and then I joined her. It would not be true to say that she was dozing. In common with most of my compatriots, I knew a *bit* about DTs—the cold turkey and the pink elephant. This was one of the shallow comas that normally precede recovery; Zoya was deeply cooperating with sleep, abandoning herself to it, breathing hungrily, and she was smooth of brow.

There must be very few women who, on a first liaison, exult in an unconscious lover. And perhaps not many men; but it has its constituency. For the time being it exactly suited my purpose. She was lying on her side, facing away; then she tipped forward and flattened herself out with a swivel of the hips.

So the inventory began. Each shoulderblade, each upper hump of her spine, each rib. After just the right amount of time she turned onto her back. From recto to verso. You see, I would be needing to know what men had done to each part of her body. I would be needing to know the history, the full picaresque, of either breast and either buttock, of these legs that had opened, of these lips that had kissed and sucked. And I was even thinking that we would both have to live for a very long time. We would both have to live long lives, Zoya and I, in order to complete our work.

Her strapless brassiere or bustier, which I had already

taken the liberty of unfastening, I now conjured out from beneath her slip. Also, by the patient application of my left kneecap, I prevailed on her thighs, which in the end slackly parted, causing the hem of the petticoat to inch up toward the whiter white.

It was now, as I continued to snuffle and rummage, that Zoya began to stir. Local tremors, originating in the calves or the forearms, would roll through the plates of her body. A faint sound issued from her, nasal, a soft whinnying; she was like a bitch all atremble in her basket, chasing cats and cars. Inside me the atmosphere was that of a very hot day in the middle of winter: warmth, gratitude, a deferred awareness of the unnatural.

I began to kiss her lips. We had done this before, after all. I had kissed her. She had kissed me. Now we kissed again.

And up she flowed from the depths, all at once, her seizing arms, her tongue flooding my mouth, the jouncing shove of her groin. I thought, with a whisper of panic: one night will not be enough. For such an inundation—one night, one year, will not begin to sustain it.

"Oh, fuck, yes," she said.

So, Venus, I had several seconds of that. I had several seconds of that. And then she opened her eyes. And awoke.

I suppose that this is the best you can say of what followed: technically speaking, it was not a rape from scratch. And it was very quick. Zoya opened her eyes and saw, inches away, a horrible delusion: it was I, Delirium Tremens. She had had the bad dream, then the good dream, then the horrible delusion. Now she had reality, and the locked shape beneath me at once gave way to infuriated struggle. But I remembered how you did it. You see, I remembered how you did it: the heavy palm over the airway, while the other hand . . . At a certain point her struggle ceased, and she pretended she was dead. It was very quick.

To understand her, in this last passage of time, please subtract from your thoughts any imputation of theatricality. Her manner wasn't even pointed; it directed you to no meaning. She was uncanny. That's what she was.

But first it was given to me to lie there, staring at the other wall, and hear her in the bathroom, hear her crash around with all the taps wrenched up, hear the rattle of the shower curtains, hear the slam of the toilet seat and its repeated flush. The door opened; and I could make out the sounds familiar to any man, as his wife or lover, in quiet self-sufficiency (and wrapped in a towel, perhaps), gathers and marshals her clothes. Then the runnel of the sliding door. Venus, the male orgasm, the male climax: only the rapist knows what a paltry thing it is. I clothed myself, and followed.

Zoya was standing in the shadows by the armchair that held her coat, her hat, her gumboots. She wore stockings and bustier and nothing else—madamlike, then, but innocent of all calculation and allure. In her raised hand she held her skirt and was wetting a finger to remove some thread or speck from its surface. As she methodically dressed herself, and then sat, back erect, to attend to her makeup, I moved around her rubbing my hands. Yes, I did try to speak; now and then I groaned out half a sentence of abjection or entreaty. Once or twice her eyes happened to pass over me, without reproach, without interest, without recognition. All that issued from her, every ten seconds or so, was a spitting sound, unemphatic but maddeningly punctual. As when a child discovers it can do something new with its mouth—hold its breath, pop its lips.

A new feeling was being born in me. At first it seemed at least vaguely familiar and, one supposed, just about manageable—no more, perhaps, than a completely new way of being very ill. I sat down at the table, under the light, and examined it, this birth. It was invisibility. It was the pain of the former person.

Fully clothed—coat, hat—she came out of the shadows. She stood in profile, an arm's reach away. A minute passed. I could tell that she was considering something, something grave; and I could tell that I myself was not in her thoughts. She took one of the long glasses and shook the water out of it. Then she poured from the squat decanter—four inches, five—and drank it all in as many swallows. Zoya shuddered to the ends of her fingers, spat, breathed out, spat again, and made for the door.

Now the gravamen. Hie thee to the dictionary—that's a good girl. Remember: every visit adds another gray cell.

. . .

Ten days later I was in Chicago. Like anyone else who had worked in state armaments, I was a "defector cat. A"—no great matter; but it took me quite a while to open up a channel to my sister, and not until March did I hear anything from home.

Her letter was written in haste, Kitty said, because my courier was sitting in the room, and staring at her, as she wrote . . . She offered wan congratulations on the success of my transposition. She went on to say that Lidya was clearing out the little house—she was moving in with her parents. There were various "effects" of Lev's that would be passed on to me, by this route, as soon as they arrived from Tyumen. Kitty said that she too was considering a change of address: she was going to live, as a paying guest, in her lover's two-room apartment. It didn't sound like a good idea, she knew, but she expected to be lonelier, now, than formerly.

As for my other sister-in-law, my sometime sister-in-law, there was, alas, "grave news." Kitty said that for months all her notes went unanswered. Her phone calls, sinisterly, were received by "a machine," and were not returned. She even went to the Embankment, and through a slit in the door had a whispered minute with the maid, who said her mistress was "unwell," was "indisposed." Kitty heard nothing until she saw it in the paper—a lone paragraph at the foot of the page. On the night of February 1, 1983, the fifty-four-year-old wife of the beloved playwright Ananias threw herself off the Big Stone Bridge. There was blood on the ice of the Moscow River.

As forgetful as ever, Zoya left some articles of clothing in my rooms at the Rossiya. The wrinkled petticoat and the torn pants I found in the bathroom trashcan. The gumboots, in their transparent polythene pouch, I found on the sitting room floor. So I was obliged to imagine her, that night, uncertain of foot in the iron rink of the capital. Zoya wasn't very steady on her legs (no mountain goat), because as a child, if you remember, she had never learned how to crawl.

PART IV

1.

From Mount Schweinsteiger to Yekaterinburg: September 4–6, 2004

Here they come, the wild dogs.

There are eight, no, nine of them, mongrels of different strains, different sizes, some shaggy, some close-coated, and all of them, like all dogs everywhere, descended from wolves. They move *slowly*, fanned out over the breadth of the alley, so that every scent can be reconnoitered, reported back on. Oh, how their noses love the smells. And there is time, too, to squat and squirt, to lay down the middens. Both sexes are represented: they are the brutes and the bitches. One is pregnant, heavy—big with the wild pups of Predposylov. She comes last, under light escort. As they approach I raise my arms to shoulder height, to make myself yet bigger. One ratlike, almost mouselike beast snarls up at me but cringes at once when I snarl back, and scurries by. I follow.

Just around the corner one of their number, on the flank, swoops down on a dropped shopping bag (of frayed straw, abandoned, perhaps, by a fleeing grandmother) and alerts the others with a shoutlike yap. Nine questing sets of jaws, nine quivering tails. But the bag contains only fruit, and they move on, one returning quickly and taking an apple in its holster-shaped snout.

As they file across the street there is a boost of speed from an accordion bus, and its front wheel strikes the gravid bitch with a sodden thud. A fierce cheer comes from the passengers (with a yodel in the middle of it, as the bus hits a pothole). The dog is dead or dying in the gutter. The others prod her with their noses, they lick her face; one tries to mount her, his back legs tense and trembling and, for a moment, meanly old-manlike. They leave her and move on. They look back, and move on.

The wild dogs of Predposylov don't look wild to me. They look trained—not by a human, but by another dog; and this superdog taught them all he knew. I no longer believe that they savaged the five-year-old in the pastel playground. The five-year-old, I conjecture, was savaged by a German shepherd belonging to the security forces, as a prelude to a riotous and scatter-fire attempt to kill every pet in Siberia.

Yes, I'm re-Russified. But what can you do? The rule is: *This thing, like every other, is not what it seems; and all you know for sure is that it is even worse than it looks.* Every Russian I talk to, without exception, tells me that Middle School Number One is the work of the government. How would it go? For reasons of state, it would begin. For reasons of state—and then, in Aesopian language, the word is handed down. For reasons of state, we need something that will strengthen national support for the war on our southeastern border. Exploding apartment blocks and airplanes aren't any good—we need something worse than that. We need a lower low.

Of course, this is just a theory. And one that betrays symptoms of paranoia, at least to Western eyes. Still, the fact that every Russian spontaneously and independently subscribes to it: *that* is not a theory.

You will think me tendentious, my dear. But this is what they look like.

The planet has a bald patch, and its central point is the Kombinat. There are no living trees in any direction for over a hundred versts. But some of the dead ones are still standing. Typically, two leafless, twigless branches remain; they point, not upward or outward, but downward, and meet at the trunk. Seen from a distance, the trees look like the survivors of a concentration camp, wandering out to be counted, and shielding their shame with their hands. Above them, the watchtowers of the cableless pylons.

You will think me tendentious. But that is what they look like.

That's what they look like from the slopes of Mount Schweinsteiger. I pace its modest gradients with my limp and my cane. Twice, now, I have postponed the flight to Yekaterinburg. There is a place I need to find, a place I need to be, before I go.

2.

Statistics, Silence, Necessity

The graph consists of two lines that toil their way from left to right. The upper line is the birth rate, and slopes downward; the lower line is the death rate, and slopes upward. They converged in 1992. Thereafter the line of life drops sharply, and the line of death as sharply climbs. It looks like a three-year-old's attempt to draw the back half of a whale or a shark: the broad torso narrows to nothing, then flairs into the tailfin. Russian cross.

Fatigue, undernourishment, cramped housing, and the nationwide nonexistence of double beds: these help. But the chief method of birth control in Russia is abortion—the fate of seven-tenths of all pregnancies. Seven-tenths of these abortions will be performed after the first trimester, and in an atmosphere of great squalor and menace; the need for further abortions is often obviated by the process (variously though inadvertently achieved) of sterilization. Failing that, there is always child mortality: the rate has improved in the last five years and is now on a par with Mauritius and Colombia.

A man in Russia is nine times more likely to die violently than a man in Israel. Failing that, he will live about as long as a man in Bangladesh. There is a new demographic phenomenon: the all-babushka village, where the young are gone and the men are dead.

It is thought that Russia could become "an epidemiological pump." The northern Eurasian plain will be girded by a cordon sanitaire, and visitors will arrive dressed like moonwalkers.

Over the next fifty years, in any event, the population is expected to halve.

There is a young family here at the hotel (they await permanent accommodation): burly husband, burly wife, small boy. They always wear tracksuits, as if expected to be ready, at the snap of a finger, for a run or an exercise drill; but all they ever do is eat. And they are silent and dedicated eaters. I sit with my back to them in the dining room. You hear nothing from their table except the work of the cutlery and the clogged or slurped requests for more—plus the faint buzzes and squeaks of the various gadgets the boy is plugged into (headphones, game console), together with the restless scraping of his illuminated rollerblades. I wonder if they ever discuss the kind of deal they have entered into. The uninterrupted ingestion of food makes it easier to maintain the silence—the conspiracy of silence.

Mother and father are destined for the Kombinat. Their natural strength will be extracted from them, as nickel is extracted from ore. Youth will be smelted out of them, and they will be duly replaced—perhaps by their son and his future bride. Wages are high. Careers are short. But now they have a health plan, and you'll be getting assistance with that respiratory disease, that early-onset tumor.

What I am seeing, I suppose, is capitalism with a Russian face, a statist face. The state has given up on nationalization and the monopoly of employment. It is now just the major shareholder, the chief oligarch—the autogarch or olicrat. And the state must continue to be hard and heavy, because topography keeps trying to tear Russia apart.

Ananias was wrong. Free men and women will come and use up their bodies in this frozen and venomous bog—at the market price. Russians will come to Predposylov. What they won't do, being Russians, is go away again. The Kombinat tries to shed them, these middle-aged gimps and wrecks. It gives them shares, valuable in Moscow, but they sell them here at the scalpers' stalls. It gives them apartments in the cities of the south, but they sell them too, and stay. You see them in the street, ready to hunker down, any day now, for a night that lasts four months.

Lev didn't *want* to come to Predposylov, though by the end, it's true, he wasn't sure he wanted to leave. The rationale for slave labor, by the way, was as follows. I was clinically speechless for a week when I found out what it was. The rationale for slave labor? It helped keep the people terrorized, and, far more importantly, it made money. But it didn't make money, it never made money. It lost money. Everyone knew this except the General Secretary. From which one concludes that there was a conspiracy of silence.

"If only someone would tell Joseph Vissarionovich." But no one ever dared.

Ananias was wrong. Ananias the widow. The widow Ananias, now of course long dead.

You and I once spent an hour on this question, for some paper of yours at CU. Do you remember? They phrased it differently, less judgmentally, of course, but here's what it amounted to: in the thirties and forties of the twentieth century, who was more disgusting, Russia or Germany? *They* were, I said. *Much* more disgusting.

But something follows from that. They were much more disgusting than we were. Still, they recovered and we did not. Germany isn't withering away, as Russia is. Rigorous atonement—including, primarily, not truth commissions and state reparations but prosecutions, imprisonments, and, yes, executions, sacramental suicides, crack-ups, self-lacerations, the tearing of hair—reduces the weight of the offense. Or what is atonement for? What does it do? In 2004, the German offense is a very slightly lighter thing than it was. The Russian offense, in 2004, is still the same offense.

Yes, yes. I know, I know. Russia's busy. There's that other feature of national life: permanent desperation. We will never have the "luxury" of confession and remorse. But what if it isn't a luxury? What if it's a necessity, a dirt-poor necessity? The conscience, I suspect, is a vital organ. And when it goes, you go.

If it was up to me, I'd demand a formal apology, in writing, for the tenth century; and for all the others in between. But no trembling relicts, made of smoke and flame, are going to rear up and wring their hands. No Russian God is going to weep and sing.

Say sorry, someone. Someone tell me they're sorry. Go on. Cry me the Volga, cry me the Yenisei, cry me the Moscow River.

3.

Spirit Level

Lev's *effects* reached Chicago in the late spring of 1983: a sizeable plywood crate, glued and pressed and nailed. It lay immured in the closet in my study for twenty-one years. Then I opened it up. The precipitant was the news of Kitty's death, and the undeniable intimations of my own. I waited for a morning that combined a faultless sky with the prospect of lunch at your apartment. Then, after breakfast, I asked the entity known as courage to take me by the hand. We went together to the toolbox for the chisel and the claw hammer. You see, one of my achievements, in the Rossiya, was the disfigurement of the past. And you don't want to look at a disfigured thing, do you, when it clearly can't be healed. This is what I was facing: testimony to the astounding dimensions of my crime—my perfect crime. I knew, too, that Lev's offering would be boobytrapped or tripwired. I knew it would explode in my face.

Well then. A leather belt, two ties, a scarf of my mother's and some more of her books, a trophy of Artem's, a clock, a straight razor, a hip flask, a spirit level (with its sleek burnish and its tragic eye), a white shoebox, and a green folder . . . The folder had a title: "Poems." The shoebox was full of photographs. I slid one out and dragged my gaze over it: me, Zoya, and Lev, at Black Lake in Kazan: 1960, and the innocent haze of monochrome. But of the three faces only hers, under its bobble hat, had the light of pleasure—pleasure in the novelty of being photographed. Lev's face was half averted, the eyes seeking something lower down and to the side. Mine was ulterior, and expressed the humorlessness of vigil: Kitty will click the camera, and another second will pass.

I rose up from the chair and strode to the desk with the green folder under my arm. It was my intention now to read the poems: the collected Lev. You must imagine my scholarly glower and the jutting lips of bookish inquiry—the abnormal normality of it, like the shrewd interest a man will suddenly take in the decor of the waiting room at his oncologist's. While I do this normal thing (I was secretly thinking), this normal thing I'm quite good at, nothing abnormal can happen to me. I sat; I breathed in through my teeth; my frowns were like push-ups of the eyebrows. Excellent, I said out loud: chronological. Here, after all, is a *life*.

Twenty-two poems covered the period from Lev's first serious efforts to his arrest in 1948 at the age of nineteen. Very Mandelstamian, I adjudged: well-made, and studiously conversational, and coming close, here and there, to the images that really hurt and connect. Too young, of course. There were poems about girls, girls in general, but no love poems.

A hiatus, now, until 1950, and then six or seven a year

until 1956. These would have been memorized at the time and written up in freedom. They were all love poems—"you" lyrics, addressed to the loved one. Let us say that these were more difficult for me to assess. They were clenched, pained, pregnant. What they assailed me with, apart from the jolts and jabs of bile and loss, was an unbearable sense of emotional deprivation. As if I had never felt anything for anyone. I just thought I had . . . The last was dated July 1956: a matter of weeks, perhaps days, before the conjugal visit in the chalet on the hill.

After that, nothing for eight years. And then the stiff-limbed, almost apologetic resumption after the birth of his son. Two decades, and a smattering of epigrams about Artem. As I worked through them, I was asking myself what it all amounted to. A raft of clever juvenilia; a body of love lyrics written in slavery; and eight haikus about fatherhood. Nine.

I hadn't been liking the look of poem number nine. It was unobjectionable in itself—a minimalist reflection on the quandary of the only child. But poem number nine had something underneath it. A rectangular presence of whiter white.

It was of course a letter, bearing my name and my old Moscow address. The envelope was sealed, and additionally fortified by a strip of sticking plaster. Not flesh-colored, but the nubby brick-red of Russian first aid. Inside were several pages. In holograph: in his small utilitarian hand.

"*Brother,*" it began. "*I said I would answer your question before I died. I'm going to keep the first half of that promise. I feel sure that I will be able to slake your curiosity. I also intend to mortify your soul. Ready yourself."*

And that was as far as I got. And that's what I've been doing ever since—readying myself.

Yes, I'll read Lev's letter. But I don't want to give it any time at all to sink in.

I'll read it later. I want that to be more or less the last thing I do.

4.

Test Tube

It was on one of my final twilit staggerings, by the side of Mount Schweinsteiger's hollowed hulk, that I found it. Here the landforms, the tectonic plates, the very points of the compass have been reshuffled and redealt, but I found it: the steep little lane, the five stone steps stacked there just for you; and then the cleared tabletop of the foothill. No buildings, now, but you could still see the ridged outlines on the ground—the outlines of the annex of the House of Meetings. I crossed the threshold. As I kicked my way through the rubble and rubbish, I heard the faint resonance of creaking glass. My shoe nosed through the shavings, and then I stooped. I held it up, the feebly glinting thing: a cracked test tube, in a wooden frame. That dark smear on its rim. Maybe it was the wildflower with its amorous burgundy, witness to an experiment in human love.

In my other hand I held a plastic bag. It didn't take very long to fill it—with femurs, clavicles, shards of skull. I was walking on a killing field. A grave churned up by bulldozers and excavators. Further around the slope I encountered a kind of sentry hut; it looked like a single-occupancy toilet, but it was in fact a *shrine*. Inside: icons, an apple, a wooden cross nailed to the wall. No, this is not a country of nuance . . . The Jews have Yad Vashem and an air force. We have a prefab and a cankered apple. And a Russian cross.

I walked back to the city square. I bought a beer and a paper, and sat on a bench before a fablon-decked table. The only other customer was a speckly man in a gypsy outfit, irrevocably slumped, thank God, over his accordion. An item at the foot of page one in the *Post* informed me that the "numbers" of Joseph Vissarionovich continue to climb. His approval rating is what a devout and handsome U.S. president might expect in a time of monotonous prosperity. With my bag of bones and my cracked test tube, I sat in a trance of lovelessness and watched it—the harlequinade. The harlequinade of the incorrigible.

The middle-aged wrecks I told you about, the ones that won't go away: a group of them, men and women, stood on the corner selling—auctioning—their analgesics to etiolated youths in overcoats made from vinyl car-seat covers. Then, very quickly, the old get drunk and the young get blocked. Twenty minutes later everyone is crashing and splashing around in the blood-colored puddles infested with iron oxide, used syringes, used condoms, American candy-bar wrappers, and broken glass. They veer and yaw and teeter. And they just watch each other drop. Yes, it's all gone—the wild dogs have more esprit. That's right, stay down. No one's going to lick your face or try and fuck you back to life.

That night was Friday, and Predposylov was smashed, not on vodka, but on surgical spirit, or *spirt*, at thirty cents a flagon. One kiosk was glass-backed, and starkly lit, like a beacon. I went over and stared at it. I stared at the comfortable figure of the blonde in her trap. All she had for sale was surgical spirit and heaped paperbacks of a single genre. That's all she was dealing in: *The Myth of the Six Million*, *Mein Kampf*, *The Protocols of the Elders of Zion*, and *spirt*. And the blonde sat idly at the cash register, her face resting on the cushion of her placid double chin, as if what encircled her (on the shelves, in the streets and in the belts all around) was completely ordinary, and not a part of something nightmarish and unforgettable . . . You know what I think? I think there must have been a developmental requirement that Russia simply failed to meet. She's not like Zoya. Russia learned how to crawl, and she learned how to run. But she never learned how to walk.

Tomorrow I fly to Yekaterinburg. I am ready. We can close, now, with two letters from the sick bay.

5.

Lev's Letter

It is dated July 31, 1982. "Brother," it begins.

I said I would answer your question before I died. I'm going to keep the first half of that promise. I feel sure that I will be able to slake your curiosity. I also intend to mortify your soul. Ready yourself.

For twenty-six years to the day I have been trying to write a long poem called "House of Meetings." A long poem. Symmetrically, though, my flame or numen, such as it was, died on that night, along with everything else. You'll eventually see that I did manage two or three stanzas, much later on. I don't think you'll find them of interest. They're about Artem, I'm afraid. They're nursery rhymes. That's all they are.

No, I couldn't do it, that poem. I couldn't tell that story. But now I'm dead, and I can tell it to you.

I am writing this in hospital. Our health system may be thick-fingered (with grimy nails), but it is broad-handed. The attitude to illness is this. All treatment—and no prevention. Still, they are using me to test the new asthma drug. I am not the first. It is clear that most, if not all, of the previous candidates suffered fatal heart attacks. Early on, too. But so far there is a concord of interests. My heart holds up and I breathe easy. How delicious air is. How luxurious to draw it in—once you know you can get the fucking stuff out. Air, even this air, with its smells of ashtrays (everyone still smokes, patients, cleaners, caterers, doctors, nurses), fierce medications, and terminal tuberculosis, tastes nice. Air tastes nice.

So—I watched her coming up the path, her walk, her shape exaggerated by the window's bendy glass. She entered. And the moment of meeting was exactly what you would want it to be. I felt the force of certain clichés—"beside myself," for example. I needed two mouths, one to kiss, one to praise. I needed four hands, one to unclip, one to unbutton, one to stroke, one to squeeze. And all the time I was replenishing memories worn thin by mental repetition. When you caress Zoya, she writhes, she almost wriggles, as if to broaden the inclusiveness of your touch. Children do that. Artem did it.

With the removal of each piece of clothing came the delivery of enormous stores of fascination. If there was an unwelcome feeling, at this stage, it was a kind of humorous mortal fear. Remember the shiteater who traded in his bowl and spoon, and then overdosed on a double ration? And who could forget the fate of Kedril the Gorger? As Zoya got more and more naked, I kept thinking about those ridiculous tsarist banquets we used to fantasize about. Salmon lips and peacock eyelids seethed in honey and burbot roe. And two hundred courses of it, with forty-five kinds of pie, and thirty different salads.

It is necessary at this point to tell you something about

Zoya's amatory style. I am not fastidious or possessive about these things (as I feel you are), and it is my intention, in any case, to encumber you—to hobble you—with confidences. Most remarkably, most alchemically, she was a big woman who weighed about half a kilo in bed. She was also very inventive, preternaturally unsqueamish, and quite incredibly long-haul. During our first nine months together, love-making, it seems fair to say, took up much of our time. For instance, with breaks for naps and snacks our last session (before the day of the marriage and my ten-minute trial) went on for seventy-two hours.

Before very long, in the House of Meetings, we were doing it—the thing that people do. I was so awed by my readiness, my capability, that it took me a while before I started asking myself what was wrong. It was this—and at first it felt entirely bathetic. As I made love, I wasn't thinking about my wife. I was thinking about my dinner. The huge chunks of bread, the whole herring, and the fat-rich broth that you and the others had so carefully and movingly amassed. Of course I could say to myself, You haven't had food in front of you and then done something else for eight years. But it would be untrue to say that I wasn't already very frightened. One of the many awful things about that night was a sense of invasion from within and the feeling that I was the mere spectator of an alien self.

We had our dinner. And bloody good it was too. And the vodka, and the cigarettes. Then I helped her wash. She had spent that day in the back of a truck, and you couldn't tell the smudges from the bruises. Two weeks on the rails and the roads. I was exulting, now, in her bravery, her fidelity, her beauty, her uncanny vivacity. God, what a *sport* she was. I was full of thanks and I was again eager.

This time I was pleased, at the outset, to find that I wasn't thinking about food. All that did, though, was delay the recognition that I was thinking about sleep. Sleep, and pity. It was one of those times when your hidden thoughts and feelings show you the results of their silent labor. You find out what's been worrying you, and how very much it's been worrying you—and with what good reason. I wanted to be pitied into sleep. That's what I wanted. And eventually we did sleep, for many hours, and at dawn we drank the tea in her flask and we began again. This time I didn't think about sleep or food or even freedom. By now I had found my subject. All I thought about was what I'd lost.

And what *was* that? I remembered the first law of camp life: to you, nothing—from you, everything. I also thought of the urka slogan (and the text of many an urka tattoo): You may live but you won't love. Now, it would be ghoulish to say that I had lost all my love. And not true, not true. This is what had happened to me, brother—I had lost all my play. All.

It may not have escaped your notice that Zoya is more attractive than I am. Why, you said as much yourself, more than once, in 1946. I can assure you that I knew it—each of my senses knew it. I had felt exalted enough by the clumsy kindnesses of my Olga, my Ada. Then *Zoya*, the grand slam of love, who cured my stutter in a single night. What next? Would she make me tall, would she kit me out with a chin and a pair of ears that matched? And, yes, she did, she did.

I felt myself revolutionized—and freed. And my response was an unbounded gratitude. I just couldn't do enough for her. Perpetual praise and infinite consideration, endearments and embraces, couplets, trinkets, messages, massages—undivided attention, together with the deployment of a desire that had no upper limit. The "specieshood" you talked about during those months of heroic madness in '53, the "earthed" feeling—what you found in the communality I had found in her. With this superlove I redressed the balance. And she would look at me, at *me*, and say she couldn't believe her luck. Oh, bro, I was almost paranoiac with happiness. It was like religion combined with *reason*. And I worshipped alone.

That night in the House of Meetings all my consciousness of inferiority returned, and it was reinforced, now, by the meaning of my enslavement. In Moscow, in the conical attic, I was Lev, but I was clean and free. I thought: she should have seen me a couple of hours ago, before the shearer and the power-hose—a little tumbleweed of nits and lice. So, to the silent but universal murmur of dismay I always heard, faintly, whenever I entered the fold of her arms, was added another voice, which said, "Never mind if he looks like a village idiot. That's their business. How about what he *is*. He is an ant that toils for the state at gunpoint. What he is is a *slave*. Nothing to be done but pity him, pity him." And I did want pity. I wanted the pity of all Russia.

Gathered about me was a raucous audience of thoughts, little gargoyles that sniggered and heckled. What was this miracle of womanliness beneath me and all around me? Women weren't meant to look like women, not anymore. Then, Christ, the business with the hands. I kept thinking, Where is the hand that killed my ear? Where are the hands of Comrade Uglik? Are my hands his hands? Are his mine? This claw of mine, this crab—whose is it? And just by being there, just by not being absent, my hands seemed heavy, violent. And behind all this was the thought that, I don't know—the thought that a man was not a good thing to be. I couldn't keep it out. No thought was so stupid or noxious that I wouldn't let it in. Because any thought whatever made a change from the other thought—the thought about what I'd lost.

I didn't expect things to be any different in freedom. And they weren't. Considered as a matter of the sensations, the nerve centers, the physical act was still far nicer than anything else I could imagine getting up to. I thought I could simply concentrate on the carnal. But when the heart goes, so, very soon, does the head. It became impossible to protect myself from the idea that what I was doing was fundamentally inane—like revisiting a futile and arduous hobby I had long outgrown. When you've lost all your play, guess what love becomes. Work. Work that gets harder every hour. Night-time was a nightshift, looming over me the whole day long. Here it comes again (with satirical touches, true, with jokes and jeers), the rambling reminder of what I'd lost. I had to search my face for the contours of tenderness, but these shapes, too, were all gone.

That night in camp I did an excellent impersonation of the old Lev—that is to say, the young Lev. But the old Lev had disappeared, along with my youth. I went on doing this impersonation for five years. And she never knew. My experience of great beauties begins and ends with Zoya, but I've invested much thought in them. In the type. I think she was very untypical sexually. Most great beauties, I suspect, tend toward the passive: mere compliance is considered bounty enough. But in another area I think she was typical—indeed, archetypical. She was not a noticer of the texture of the feelings of the people around her. Great beauties, they don't have to do the work that we have to do, the work of vox populi and "Mass Observation." Except when its content was violent, she hardly even noticed anti-Semitism. People would look at her with that compassionate sneer, as if she was a cat that had lost all its hair. Take it from me, I really got to know about the influenza of the xenophobe. It is a mirror the size of the Pacific—an ocean of inadequacies.

No, she never knew. There was only one thing I couldn't control, and it bothered her. I cried in my sleep. I was always crying in my sleep. And it was always the same dream. She used to question me about it as she dressed for work. I told her the dream was a dream about Uglik. It wasn't true. The dream was a dream called House of Meetings.

My double-goer, my antic twin, my Vadim, was still there, in freedom, and he had a plan. His plan was for me to become even uglier. Hence the beergut, the new twitch, the conscientious gracelessness—and, of course, the way I lay down or bent over for my stutter. By then I was thirsting for illness, for incapacity. I wanted to be surrounded by people dressed in white. The word hospital took on the sacred glow it had had in Norlag. All the time, now, I was aware of a "waiting" feeling. It was the impatience to be old. Previously, at the very crest of sexual bliss, I used to feel I was being tortured by someone infinitely gentle. Now I felt like that every time she smiled at me or took my hand. The last and final phase, which introduced a whole new order of alarm, presented itself in the summer of 1962. And the first symptom was physical.

I began to hear, on and off, a taut hum—like the sound of jet engines heard from within the plane. White noise, I assumed, from my dead ear. After a time I realized that it was only happening in certain situations: crossing high bridges, on clifftops and balconies, near railway lines and busy roads—and also when I shaved with the straight razor. Then one day, in Kazan, it took me half an hour to walk past a stationary truck I saw on the street. It was a garbage-compactor. The men were leaving it running as they went ever further for their loads, of course (in case it didn't start up again), and the hum in my ear was so loud that the foul mastications of the machine, its chomping and grinding, were actually noiseless, even when I came up close and stared in. The steel blocks that climbed and plunged were no more than lightly smeared, and the black teeth had almost picked themselves clean. It looked all right in there. And it made no sound.

When we were growing up you used to say I was a solipsist, and a solipsist of unusual briskness and resolve. You spoke of the sobriety of the calculation of my own interest, the lack of any instinct for compliance with the mood of the group (plus the off-center protrusion of the lower lip and the "privacy" of the eyes). Well, it remained true that I very much didn't want to kill myself. That felt like a reasonable priority. The suicide of the slave survivor—we know it's common enough, and in the end I think I can respect it. As a way of saying that my life is *mine* to take. But I thought I had held myself together fairly well, in camp—no violence, not much compromise, no herd emotion. I didn't want to do what others did. And I reckoned I had a good chance of getting through life without killing *anyone*.

In fact it all felt pretty much involuntary. I mean my strike, sudden and unofficial—the wildcat strike. I let my hands fall to my sides. Not just the nightly act, but everything else, all the smiles and sacraments, all the words, all the commentary of love. She noticed *that*. I ask you to imagine what it was like to lie there, sit there, stand there, and watch. It was quick—I'll say that. Within a month she got caught, in blazing crime, with the PT-instructor during the lunch break. And I was free.

Just to finish my side of it. I didn't want a child with

Zoya and I didn't want a child with Lidya. But it's curious. With Lidya, with *Lidya*, I felt a brief renewal of erotic purpose. There was now the possibility, at least, of a consequence. Something like—if it isn't play, then let it be earnest. And, incidentally, I've always been amazed by what Lidya thinks a fuck is, compared to what Zoya thought a fuck was. But it worked out. The boy, when he came, began to give me the sort of pleasure I used to take in Zoya. Proximity to physical grandeur, but manageable, now. I have enough love in me for Lidya, I can scrape it together and eke it out with things like approbation and respect. Lidya understands. After Zoya, I feel as if I'm living with a dedicated psychotherapist—and mindreader. I can sense her decoding my silences. She understands, and she pities me. In the end you finish with self-pity. It's too tiring. You want someone else to do it for you. Lidya pities me. She pities me, which Zoya rightly never did, and she pities me for Zoya, too.

Forcing her out, forcing Zoya out, was not a contained cruelty. No one knew better than I did how hopeless she was at love. The awful way she laid herself open. She was a totalist among men who dealt in fractions. I know you and Kitty were appalled by her marriage, but I was secretly ecstatic, for a while, anyway. The irony is very sharp, I agree. But bear in mind that she was hopeless at other things too, including money. In the few months between our separation and our divorce she ran up debts that looked like state budgets. I heard that in the end it cost Ananias half of all he had to bail her out. At last: reparation. The money earned by mocking the sweat of slaves—it goes to Zoya. Hereafter, or so I felt, that dreadful old piece of shit will keep her warm and fed and clothed, and will value her. Or so I felt.

Now, my brother. It is my suspicion that you aren't yet done with Zoya. You're going to wait until after I'm dead and then you're going to try again. Not immediately after. I don't see you getting on the plane with a suitcase in one hand and a funeral baked meat in the other. Listen. There was one night in Moscow, the time we stayed over, and you'd been giving her "that look" every five minutes—you think you're all strong and silent, bro, but you're a book with its spine cracked open and its pages falling free. We were talking about it as we went to bed. I said, as was my habit, "Like a clever dog that knows it's going to be thrashed." Now you remember how perceptive she could be, when she tried, when she stopped and thought. I'll indent her reply, to give it extra weight:

> No, not anymore. More like a dog on a leash. With a gendarme at the other end of it. He lusts, but he also hates. See the way he's always having a dig at Varvara about her past. You'd think he'd delivered her from prostitution. I bet he tortures her. That's what he'd do to me. An endless exercise. An endless wank about the past. About you. You and all the others.

And you know what she did then? She made the sign of the cross. She.

Given a world of free will, you would have no chance with

Zoya, not a prayer. It's very simple: you're violent. In camp, when I went pacifist, that was an attempt to preserve something in myself. It's the philosophy of the truant, I know—of the pious shirker. I assumed at the time that you were doing some discreet brawling on my behalf, and I stayed silent. I remember the change in the attitude, and the appearance, of the three little hooligans who were always after me. They looked as though they'd all been in the same car crash. Christ. And that Tartar who wanted my shovel—was it you who broke his arm? Anyway, I tried, with my share of hypocrisy, to preserve something in myself. It didn't work. Nothing would have worked. And I don't condemn you, really, for what you did—to the informers. Oppression lays down bloodlust. It lays it down like a wine.

Now I know you to be a persistent and resourceful suitor—and, in her case (if I may say), a remarkably sanguine one. But she is weak against certain kinds of influence. And if the old hack is still alive, when I'm not, and she is still with him, well, it already sickens me to imagine her isolation, and her thwartedness. This I feel sure of, though, and I warn you with real fear. If you do move on her, it will create for you both nothing but misery. Not to mention, or at least not to go into, the insult it would in any case be to my memory, and to our fraternal love. A love that survives the strangest fact of all.

You wanted me dead, didn't you? From pretty much the first day I came to camp. You fought it, and you won, and you risked much physical damage to keep me from harm.

Yet you wanted me dead. Because Zoya was impossible so long as I was alive. I don't know why. I don't know what urka-like rule you were following, though I'm glad of it. Or maybe you realized that I just couldn't let it happen. We'd need pistols at dawn. And then you'd get your wish. My suicide would have been simplest, no? Sometimes I find myself thinking that the entire Norlag Rebellion, the Fifty Days, with its hundred dead, was engineered by you for just one last roll of the dice. I could go, you could go—let fate do it. And, Jesus, August 4, with its deaths and its wounds. Wounds that turned our friend's hair from taiga to tundra. As I said at the time, you're a romantic. In your way. And no fun for you either, all this. No fun to want your brother's wife. And to want her quite so badly.

What I'd like to do is live long enough so that you're too old to care. Or too old to move. You'll realize how serious I am when I tell you that I'm going to give up smoking. But I don't see them, really, the old bones. Who was it who said this? "In hospital, it's always earlier than you think." Earlier—and also later, at least for me. On my admission, they had me sign a form that said, more or less, that I didn't mind dying. I've made my will, and I'm already dividing up my keepsakes, like the good little boy I used to be. Oh, what good boys we were. What good boys we were, before. The delivery of this letter I will entrust to Artem, whose tour ends at Christmas. It's the only trait my wives have in common: you can't ask them to post a letter. You might as well fold the envelope into a paper plane and throw it out of the window. And I don't expect Lidya to be at her briskest, after I've gone.

You know what happened to us, brother? It wasn't just a compendium of very bad experiences. The hunger and the cold and the fear and the boredom and the oceanic weariness—that was general, and standard-issue. That was off the rack. What I'm referring to is the destiny that is made to measure. Something was designed inside us, blending with what was already there. For each of us, in different ways and settings, the worst of all possible outcomes, and a price to be paid, not by the spoonful or the shovelful, but by the dayful, the yearful, the lifeful. They did more than take our youth away. They also took away the men we were going to be. Watching Uglik, our master, trying to light his second cigarette—that's when I felt it growing in me, my specific deformation.

What's yours? Mine is cynicism. I've risen above it here and there in this letter to you, but the tone I use in speaking of the mother of my son is evidence enough of how it's gone with me. Cynicism is what I feel, or what I don't feel, all the time. And who would be a cynic? Cynic. Dogface. Condemned to see cynicism everywhere. But it's here. It has me. I don't care about anything or anyone. Blindspots, susceptibilities, come and go. I can sometimes persuade myself that I don't care about Lidya, Kitty, you, Mother. I can seldom successfully convict myself of the blasphemy of not caring about Artem. And I can never say that I don't care about Zoya.

Again—what's yours? Only you have the right to name it. I used to think it was the war, and not camp, that fucked you up. But you won the war. And nobody won the other thing. Still, whatever the war did, camp trapped it inside you. For both of us, I think, it had to do with our weakened power to love. It is strange that enslavement should have that effect—not just the fantastic degradation, not just the fear and the boredom and all the rest, but also the layered injustice, the silent injustice. So all right. We're back where we started. To you, nothing—from you, everything. They took it from me, it seems, for no reason other than that I valued it so much. And maybe the brutes and the bitches had the truth of it. Those sore letters on Arbachuk's stiff-veined forearm. You may live but you won't—

I wish you well. It's a great relief to be able to say that, and to mean it. I don't wish many people well, not anymore. All the people I don't know—I no longer wish them well. Tales of infirmity and destitution: that's the kind of thing, these days, that very slightly cheers me up. Just now, I am having one of my better moments. I feel disencumbered. And I hope you do what I did, and manage to patch together some family around you. Good luck. And thanks. Thanks for the hefty loan, thanks for my Certificate of Manumission, and thanks for the seat on the train, that time. And, yes, thanks for breaking the Tartar's arm. Boy, you were something. The way you'd make the German shepherd cringe and go belly-up and pee. "You think I'm going to be sneered at," you told it, "by a fucking dog?" And in the last months of the war, the cannonades in Moscow whenever a major city fell—with every boom I felt your power.

You know, without your influence on Vad, I don't think I would have survived childhood. That Vadim. On the strength of the fact that he came out first, he took on all the wants and wounds of the older brother. He <u>really</u> wanted me dead. And he wasn't just going to hope for the best: he was going to do something about it. Why? Because I spoiled that blood-smeared half-hour idyll—when he had his mother all to himself. Ever since I was born, you were my righter. My righter of wrongs. You towered like a god—you straddled the ocean, you filled the sky. And I still feel that. Having you for a brother was like having a hundred brothers. And so it will always be. Lev.

Oh, slave, thou hast slain me . . .

Yes, that's right. Yes, that's right, my girl. It was not your finest hour. In the space of it (our dinner at the Grill, late July) you subjected me to two rank vulgarisms—two craven borrowings, that is to say, from the common pool of catchphrase, ditty, and jingle. Don't "go there," Venus. Do not enter that necropolis of novelty.

The first was "closure." Why didn't I seek "closure"? "Closure": ech, if I so much as whisper it or mouth it I feel myself transformed into a white-coated, fat-necked peanut in a mall-style consulting-room. Closure *is a greasy little word which, moreover, describes a nonexistent condition. The truth, Venus, is that* nobody ever gets over anything. *Your second enormity was not a lone epithet: it went on for an entire sentence. "Whatever doesn't kill you makes you stronger." Not so! Not so. Whatever doesn't kill you doesn't make you stronger. It makes you weaker, and kills you later on.*

Of course, I happen to be taking the matter into my own hands. That lumbering but capacious health service Lev talked about—that's all disappeared. Only a slim majority of state hospitals can boast of running water, and I say with tears of pride that the place I'm in is one of them. When it comes to death, though, Russia remains a land of opportunity: the lethal injection, here, would be a bargain at double the price. And there's none of that right-to-life bullshit, no pious politicos or meddling divines, no crowds in the forecourt yelling at everyone to Let Me Live.

I'm in an immune-deficiency hospice (the only such unit in the country); to use the euphonious local acronym, it's for people with SPID. This unacknowledged epidemic, by the way, is of African proportions. Some time later on (they can't say when) I will be moved into a private room for my shot. And I'm wondering: how much should I tip, and when? I know. While I'm complaining. While I'm acting up: that's the time to do it. The lethal injection will work—I don't doubt that. But I am by no means persuaded that the transition will be painless. Morphine is extra, and I've ordered a double. But you're right: I should have gone to Oslo or Amsterdam and done it business-class and not economy. Still, that wouldn't answer. I am going to die where my brother died.

Call me a literalist, but I'm only doing what Russia is doing. And she tried it once before. Russia tried to kill herself in the 1930s, after her first decade of Joseph Vissarionovich. He was already a cadaver millionaire about ten times over, even before the Terror. But he did need Russians to go on producing Russians. And they stopped. After the startling census of 1936, the state jolted into action: crash kindergartenization, maternity medals, a resolemnized marriage ceremony, the legalization of inheritance, and the criminalization of abortion. It was a general strike, of a kind; and the state broke it. What will the state do now?

As the Babylonians were leading the Jews into captivity they asked them to play their harps. And the Jews said, "We shall work for you, but play we shall not." That's what they were saying in 1936, and that's what they're saying now. We will work for you, but we're not going to fuck for you anymore. We are not going to go on doing it, making people. Making people to be set before the indifference of the state. We are not going to play.

Oh, I'm not suggesting that it's died out entirely—sexual intercourse. About a third of those specters in the TV room here (former people, of the former nation) can claim to have come by their SPID through venereal means. And how else do you explain all the used condoms you see in the street? There are always these diehards and bitter-enders. Why, look at the figures for syphilis among teenage girls—an increase, over the past ten years, of fourteen thousand percent.

I can't be expected, at this stage, to change my ways. I mean my weakness for pedagogy. You have my list for further reading. They're mostly memoirs, you'll find—the memoirs of Russian slaves. I hope you read the one written, much later on, and from Iowa City, by Janusz. It is sometimes said that these books are "unrepresentative," because they all derive from the same stratum: the intelligents. *All politicals; no snakes or leeches, no brutes, no bitches. The authors are unrepresentative in another way too, in that their integrity, it seems, was never in the slightest danger. They lived; and they also loved, I think. Stakhanovites of the spirit, "shock" seekers and seers, they didn't even hate. None of this was true for my brother and me. And hate is weary work. You hate hating—you come to hate the hate.*

Let me tell you what I loved about August 4, 1953, when we stood arm in arm. When we stood and faced the state and its whirlwind of iron. I had reached the end of philosophy: I knew how to die. And men don't *know how to do that. It might even be that all the really staggering male exertions, both great and base, are brought on by this single incapacity. No other animal is asked to form an attitude to its own extinction. This is horribly difficult for us, and may be thought to mitigate our general notoriety . . . You need mass emotion—to know how to die. You need to be like all the other animals, and run with the herd. Ideology gives you mass emotion, which is why Russians have always liked it. I've gone on a bit about yours—your ideology. And all your life I've tried to interest you in* my *ideology: the ideology of no ideology. It's not a bad one, your one; but it's an ideology. And it's the only thing I detect in you that remains imperfectly free.*

I have just had a visitor. She came with fruit and flowers: little Lidya. Not so little anymore, true (the usual Slavic slab, with something religious, Quakerish, in her bulk), yet I was briefly cheered by how vigorous she seemed. She's in her mid-sixties; and don't forget that Russian women live about twenty-five percent longer than Russian men (they get the full four quarters, and not just the three). I didn't tell Lidya what I was here for exactly, but she understood that this was our last goodbye. She asked if she might say a prayer for me, and I said all right, on the assumption that I could probably bear it. I was quite wrong about that, and almost immediately started shouting her down. Not that *ideology; I wasn't going to lie there and watch her kiss the Russian cross. She apologized quite prettily, and stroked my brow, and backed out of the room. Yes, I'm in the room now. The room in the basement, with its two boilers and its thousands of pink and blue towels stacked on duckboards and smelling of vinegar. My sister-in-law will prepare another hardboard crate, and send you my PC, wallet, glasses, watch, my wedding ring and spirit level, and one or two of my clothes—a tie, a handkerchief. I gave Lidya the straight razor and the folder of poems.*

There's a final gender difference I will draw your attention to, if I may. Prepare yourself for some good news. In 1953 I discovered how to die. And now I've forgotten again. But I do know this. Women can die gently, as your mother did, as my mother did. Men always die in torment. Why? Toward the end, men break the habit of a lifetime, and start blaming themselves, with full male severity. Women break a habit too, and start blaming themselves no longer. They forgive. We can't do that. And I mean all men, not just old violators like me—great thinkers, great souls, even they have to do it. The work of who did what, and to whom.

What was the matter with me and women? On the plane, this morning, I engaged the search engine: "retrospective sexual jealousy." Lots of sexual stuff, and lots of jealousy stuff, and lots of stuff about retrospectives. I toiled past a few thousand entries—and finally came to a stylish essay from the august British journal Mind and Body*. It was called "Retrospective Sexual Jealousy and the Repressed Homosexual." With the RSJ-merchant, the essay argues, it's not the women he's interested in—it's the men. In other words, I'm crypto-queer. What makes me doubt this? Only the fact that I wouldn't have minded, much, being queer in the first place. All right, I wouldn't have liked it, in camp, taking my spoon and bowl and joining the passives, who ate at a separate table (and could only talk among themselves). After that, though, in the city, if you're not making children anyway, what's the difference? I know* you *wouldn't think the less of me. But it's probably worse, in my case, because I was queer for my brother.*

The thing that stays with me from those hours at the Rossiya, perhaps surprisingly, is an irreducible sense of the sterile. In the last months of the war, when I raped in uniform—we were, by then, so full of death (and the destruction of everything we had and knew) that the act of love, even in travesty, felt like a spell against the riot of murder. And you could people a good-sized city, now, with the by-blows of the rapist army (population: one million). Many of the impregnated women, of course, never did give birth: they were killed then and there by their rapists. I can at least truthfully say that this phenomenon was and is beyond my understanding.

And in the Rossiya? What I did had no meaning. It was gratuitous, it was perverse, and it was dedicated to the propagation of misery, but it wasn't even particularly Russian. Except maybe in this. No power, no freedom, no responsibility, ever, in all our history. It stirs an anarchy within. But no—I give it up. I said earlier that rape made a reckoning with me. Its revenge wasn't commensurate or anything like that, but it was thorough, and dramatically swift. Have you guessed? Have you asked your mother's ghost? At the Rossiya, I crossed over from satyr to senex in the course of an afternoon. As early as the next day I couldn't even remember what it was I liked about women and their bodies. I have remembered now. Over these past few days I have remembered.

Of course, it would be nice to be able to blame it, the rape, on the war or on the camp or on the state. I do honestly think, sometimes, that Artem's death (the manner of it), as well as Lev's, had overthrown my sanity. In that moment, when her wide smile of love became a gape of horror, I experienced a disappointment, *Venus, that was a thousand ply. After all that, I thought. And for just long enough the possession of Zoya felt like a right. And I didn't even have the right to be there in the room. And now when I close my eyes I can only see a moribund murderer, implacable to his last breath, gathering himself for one last thrust. It used to be an inkling and is now a conviction which perhaps you already share: in the four or five seconds between my kiss and her awakening, Zoya was dreaming about Lev. It had to be that way, to crystallize his fate and mine. Christ, Russia is the nightmare country. And always the compound nightmare. Always the most talented nightmare.*

And from this dream I am about to escape. They have come. Two men in street clothes, with what looks like a toolbox. They're having a smoke while I finish this. And so am I. Any moment now I will click SEND . . . Go, little book, go, little mine tragedy. And you go, too, Venus, go out into it, with your good diet, your lavish health insurance, your two degrees, your languages, your property, and your capital. The insane luxury of having you to think about has kept me alive, until now, anyway. And oh my heart, every time you called me Dad or Pop or Father, oh, every single time. Well, kid, it wouldn't be right to sign off sounding sour. Let's not submit to the gloom supposedly so typical of the northern Eurasian plain, the land of compromised clerics and scowling boyars, of narks and xenophobes and sweat-soaked secret policemen. Join me, please, as I look on the bright side. Russia is dying. And I'm glad.

ACKNOWLEDGMENTS

I owe a debt to several recent books.

First, Anne Applebaum's magisterial *Gulag: A History* (Allen Lane; Doubleday). Lucidly and elegantly constructed, simply and strongly written, and asking all the right questions, this is the single indispensable work, after Solzhenitsyn's *Gulag Archipelago*, on the phenomenon of Soviet slavery.

With Andrew Meier's *Black Earth: Russia After the Fall* (HarperCollins), you only have to look at the jacket photo of the author to know what lies ahead of you: honesty, intrepidity, wit, candor, and (a vital quality, hereabouts) cheerful unfastidiousness. This book combines travel writing and historiography at a formidably high level.

Orlando Figes's *Natasha's Dance: A Cultural History of Russia* (Penguin; Metropolitan Books). I have an informal method of evaluating tomes of this kind (729 pp.): I look to see how many notes I have made at the back of them (e.g., "39—serf theaters and orchestras . . . 552—Nabokov Sr.'s murderer"). My edition of *Natasha's Dance* ends, generously, with ten blank sides. I needed them all.

Like Anne Applebaum's *Gulag*, Simon Sebag Montefiore's *Stalin: The Court of the Red Tsar* (Weidenfeld & Nicolson;

Knopf) is partly the result of heroic labor in the newly opened archives. This book changes the picture, and in a disturbing way. The author is very meticulous and very moral; but he can't prevent the emergence of a Stalin more personally impressive than we generally believed him to be—more complex and more intelligent. Stalin was in possession of a certain amount of political poetry; he was also, alas, in possession of a soul.

Masha Gessen's *Ester and Ruzya* (Dial Press) has an informative subtitle: *How My Grandmothers Survived Hitler's War and Stalin's Peace*. The family memoir is very smoothly assembled; but the experience of reading it is necessarily jagged and gaunt. Gessen is superlatively good at showing how state systems bend and tug the individual into all kinds of strange shapes. She is also especially evocative on the physical furniture and mental atmosphere of postwar Moscow.

As is Janusz Bardach, in *Surviving Freedom: After the Gulag* (University of California Press). In an earlier book of mine (*Koba the Dread*) I praised an earlier book of his (*Man Is Wolf to Man: Surviving Stalin's Gulag*); Dr. Bardach wrote to me, and we had a brief interchange in the months before his death. I knew the defector-historian Tibor Szamuely, who served time at Vorkuta. But Tibor died thirty years ago. And it was Janusz Bardach whom I felt to be my one human link to the events I describe in *House of Meetings;* and in my struggle, as I wrote it, I was greatly sustained by his ghost.

And by other ghosts—by Fyodor Dostoevsky, by Joseph Conrad, by Eugenia Ginzburg, and by the Tolstoy of the USSR, Vasily Grossman.

A NOTE ON THE TYPE

The text of this book was set in Van Dijck, a modern revival of a typeface attributed to the Dutch master punchcutter Christoffel van Dyck, c. 1606–69. The revival was produced by the Monotype Corporation in 1937–38 with the assistance, and perhaps over the objection, of the Dutch typographer Jan van Krimpen. Never in wide use, Monotype van Dijck nonetheless has the familiar and comfortable qualities of the types of William Caslon, who used the original Van Dijck as the model for his famous type.

Composed by Stratford Publishing Services,
Brattleboro, Vermont
Printed and bound by R. R. Donnelley & Sons,
Harrisonburg, Virginia
Designed by Peter A. Andersen